in berkeley's green and pleasant land

in berkeley's green and pleasant land

*Songs of Innocence,
Songs of Experience*
– WIlliam Blake

stories by
Renee Blitz

REGENT PRESS
2002

*The characters in this book are entirely fictional
and any resemblance to persons living or dead
is entirely coincidental.*

Copyright © 2001 Renee Blitz-Moskowitz

Library of Congress Cataloging-in-Publication Data

Blitz, Renee, 1931 -
   In Berkeley's green and pleasant land : stories / by Renee Blitz.
     p. cm.
   ISBN 1-58790-011-4
   1. Berkeley (Calif.)-- Fiction. 2. Women--California--
Berkeley--Fiction.

PS3602.L58 15 2001
813'.6--dc21   2001019833

Manufactured in The United States of America
REGENT PRESS
6020-A Adeline
Oakland, CA 94608
www.regentpress.org

To my husband, Moe
lover-impressionist
anarchist-innocent
a million years ahead of your time

"For the world, which seems
To lie before us like a land of dreams
So various, so beautiful, so new,
Hath really neither joy, nor love, nor light,
Nor certitude, nor peace, nor help for pain . . ."
– Matthew Arnold
Dover Beach

Table of Contents

I will not cease from mental fight,
 Nor shall my sword sleep in my hand,
Till we have built Jerusalem
 In England's green and pleasant land.
  – William Blake

in berkeley's green and pleasant land   *9*

the participant   *33*

make haste, my beloved   *58*

at 15, he had been a leader in   *68*

two women   *80*

death to the fascist-imperialist dogs   *101*

the unuseable talent   *127*

notes from the tower of menopause   *152*

p.s. your thing is sticking out   *170*

the small revelation   *190*

she had mastered the art   *207*

the mother's wasteland   *213*

lies   *229*

this picnic you're having   *250*

in berkeley's green and pleasant land

Isabel knew him when she was a young girlchild in graduate school. As for him, he was an older man, probably in his late thirties, getting older of course. He was bald and fat and he looked real old to Isabel. Attached to the university in Berkeley's green and pleasant land, much as a loose tooth is attached to someone's gums, he couldn't really get his foot in anywhere. He was supposed to have been very brilliant once, in economics, he was certainly too old for all that now, who can make a stir as somebody very brilliant when they're that age? The real truth is the professors resented him because he was an unattractive, middle-aged upstart. The old professors favored the young men, and the young professors felt he was pitiful and a sad character, so John, that was his name, John just kept plugging along in his life, drinking beer and laughing his own unmistakable, hysterical, very loud laugh in the greasy student bars around town. And that's where Isabel knew him from. She'd run into him in one of the greasy cafes around school, and they would give each other that high sign they had, a friendly hug, because they had "an affinity." She was only a girlchild, on her first marriage, 24 years old.

Her husband had been stationed in Berlin during the Korean War and for 14 months she hadn't seen him. When he came back home, he confessed that he had had a "thing" with a girl, a German girl who was very young and very beautiful and very desperate and very poor, and he had lost his soul to this girl, who had had exceptionally beautiful skin as well. Isabel, who had married at 19, and had counted the days till her first and only love came home, spent many nights crying and sobbing and being so choked up she couldn't breathe. And that's what made them leave New York and come out to California and try graduate school in the first place. Her husband signed up for the GI Bill and graduate school, and she, Isabel, signed up for graduate school too.

She was a girlchild, and this John we're talking about, he was a disillusioned middle-aged man, on his fourth marriage. His marriage was full of drinking and people coming over to drink more, and many ugly, private and public drunken scenes. Isabel, for her part, spent many nights at home crying. All red-nosed and haggard from these bouts and seizures, looking very inelegant and unsvelte, she would plead for a "relationship" from her runaround husband. "Why don't you love me? Why don't we communicate?" she would beg, with her red nose and her messed up hair and her ruby-red eyes and her disheveled face. Who would guess that this fresh-looking, virginal girl, sauntering through coffee shops, could look so rotten and ugly at home, who could guess? Max, her husband, had his theories and his ways, she needs to suffer and torment herself, he told people.

John and Isabel greeted each other in their way and they were warm together. He asked her what she was studying and she said she didn't know, she had changed so many times, back and forth from English Literature to Philosophy to Comparative Literature and back again to English before she finally dropped out of graduate school altogether. She couldn't quite be a graduate student, she always lay at home brooding. "How come I'm not loved, how come I'm not famous? How come I'm not Tennessee Williams or Arthur Miller?" But everyone thought she was just too brainy to do well in the Establishment, and they all thought she was home getting brainier, exercising those brains of hers.

One day, John was in the greasy spoon cafe and Isabel came in . . . he looked very heavy and very depressed and very Armenian (which he was) and he had dark jowls and messed up eyebrows on his face and a big fur winter hat on, and he looked isolated as all hell and weighed down with fatness. She, in the meantime, had been "sauntering" around the Avenue looking for someone to have coffee with.

"I'm going to do something new," he said.

"What's that?" she asked.

"I don't know if I wanna tell anybody."

"Oh come on John, you can tell me."

"I'm going to start selling freezers," he said.

"Why, that's wonderful, that's absolutely wonderful," she said, because she was 24 .... and a literature major, and she thought anything anyone did was wonderful.

He had a wife, and his wife was an engineer, one of the few women engineers in all of California and she made a lot of money.

"I think it's time for me to make a little money," he said. "Doreen makes it designing aeronautical shit, and I gotta make it some way, so I'll sell freezers," and he laughed the hysterical laugh.

"I know," she said, but really, she didn't know the half of it because she was just a young girl who happened to be at the university when he was at the university, but really, she knew nothing about him and how he lived.

"I know what you mean," she said.

"Do you really?" and he laughed so fitfully, really, he had such a big, hysterical laugh.

"Well, of course, she said, in her disturbed 24th year, "everybody must come up with some kind of ego energy, even if it's only once in a while," and he laughed and laughed, and all the people at the table thought she was so conceptual, yes, that was it, conceptual not poetic, and it came across so well because she was such a girlchild, and the table all nodded and laughed, and she was acknowledged to be the Emily Dickinson of the cafe, unfit for life really, but bright, bright, conceptual and bright, inexperienced really in the ways of frigidaires and freezers, but with that precocious young girl "sensitivity," yes, that's what they called it then.

One other time, she went out to his house. It was a Saturday night, and he was giving a party way out in the square suburban community where he lived, bordering the university. It was a large, expensive house with a swimming pool. And it was filled with heavy drinkers. When Isabel came through the door, she saw his wife, who looked so old to her, and she was carrying on some scene. That wife, she had big hips and an older woman's dress on and full breasts, and the girlchild Isabel felt so glad that she didn't have those hips and that dress and those big breasts.

She sat down very quietly in the middle of the ugly crossfire because there was no where else to be, terribly out of her element. Max, her husband, got right into it, on the other hand, because he loved "the zanies" as he called them, but Isabel just sat there like a girl with a lute in a Medieval tapestry, except she had no lute and this was no tapestry. John's wife, Doreen, continued to act hysterical and sexual. The grown up folks were all at play, drinking, confronting and acting savage.

"Why are you sitting there on the edge of the sofa like that, honey?" said Doreen to her, "why bother to come to a party if all you're gonna do is act like that? Come on, have a drink, it won't kill you!" said the wife Doreen to the girlchild Isabel.

"I don't drink," she said.

"Come on, loosen up, it's not a funeral, it's a party!"

Finally, the party was over and they rode back home in droves of car pools to the college town, away from suburbia. He was so mortified that he had a house here, and that it had beige wall to wall carpeting and a few cream colored sofas. He told you as soon as he met you, "I have a house in suburbia, with a swimming pool yet. My wife's an engineer, and what's more, she's successful, she makes a ton of money." And when he got drunk, he'd always say, "goddamnit, I'm gonna get out of suburbia if it's the last thing I do. If it's the only thing I do!" And he would laugh and laugh.

Isabel the girlchild came home after that party and in the weeks to come she wrote what she called a 20th century morality play, using that party as a model. She loaded it with snatches of conversation she had overheard at the party, and it sounded a little like TS Eliot, with all the unconnected conversations. She worked on it a long time, telling people she was writing a morality play, a 20th century morality play, and she got a reputation for being a serious writer, but really, she was just an unhappily-married young woman girl-child now, her husband had gone ape chasing ass around the university.

The next time she saw him, they were both older.

She was still married to the same husband, Max, but she was thirty now and living in a room in a roominghouse, they were both collecting unemployment. Next door to them there was a girl named Flo Schwartz who came from a rich family with Hollywood money, but Flo was too idealistic to accept any money from them because they had made millions producing grade B movies. Flo always had tears in her eyes whenever she looked at anybody, she seemed to know how caught we all were, how trapped, and she spent her whole time crying for the human condition. She worked in the cafeteria scooping out mashed potatoes for the students every night, and wrote forty-page poems about quiet desperation. She and Isabel were close friends at this time.

One day, Max found John, penniless and laughing in a cafe, and brought him home, John must've been 46 by then. He had come back to Berkeley, divorced for the fourth time, with no job, no future, no family, and alcoholic prospects. He had gotten fatter, and more alcoholic and his laugh was louder and more hysterical than it had ever been. Max brought John up to the roominghouse, and generous, idealistic Flo agreed to put John up in her room.

At this time, Isabel was hanging around with a boy-poet named Vincent. He had a shaved-head and obsessed . . . about Indians, long before anyone ever mentioned Indians as heroes. He was also a religious fanatic on the subject of design, saying . . . design is the key to the creation of higher consciousness. So far as visual reality is concerned, or, "the visuals," as Vincent called them, they determined the level of consciousness in the perceiver. He prophesied that a whole new group of spiritual cadre, in the form of avant-garde designers, would come forth to lead us all to higher consciousness. Vincent did not walk in the ordinary way, he believed you had to "twirl" down the street, disarranging your senses as much as possible, so you could make contact with the truth. He and Isabel would twirl down the street together, Vincent, the boy-poet, and Isabel, the girlchild, and he would illustrate his cosmic ideas to her while they both twirled. He also played around with the salt and pepper shakers in the pool-hall restaurant, making them twirl as well, to further illustrate his theories. Of course, they never fucked. Isabel never did that with anyone, she just lived in her mind, because she was a girlchild. But Vincent liked her, all these people needed someone they could twirl around and feel innocent with.

One night they had been out twirling at two in the morning.

"Let's go get some chili," said Vincent.

"Let's," said Isabel.

"Let's go visit Flo," he said.

When they knocked on Flo's door, there was John, without his shirt on, standing around Flo's kitchen. Vincent walked over to him with his raggedy white pants, he always wore white to protest his innocence, his incorruptibility.

"What you doin', man?" said Vincent, his white pants stained with chili sauce.

"I'm just here.. walkin' around Flo's kitchen at three in the morning," John said, laughing.

They all laughed.

"I dig you without your shirt on," said Vincent. "Why don't we all take off our clothes?"

"Sure, if everybody wants to. How about you Isabel, what do you say?" John said.

"It's all right with me," she said.

Vincent was the first to get his pants off. He didn't wear underwear, and besides, he was adept at being naked. John was the opposite. Very self-consciously, he took off his pants and folded them up. Flo took off her clothes and promptly got a splinter in her toe, Vincent tried getting it out for her with a needle. Isabel sat and watched all this.

"You're the only one with clothes on," said John, coming over to her. "You talk big, but when it comes down to it, you're chicken. Why don't you take off your clothes?" he said.

"I don't want to," said Isabel.

"You always make people do things, but you don't do

them yourself."

They were the two oldest people in the room that time. Everybody else was 20, but Isabel was 29, and John, well, he was 46.

Finally, one day, Isabel was pregnant. She had gotten pregnant by Max in the little room in the student boarding house, down the hall from Flo. She was still unhappy in her marriage though, and she started seeing an emigré analyst that Vincent was seeing, a walk across town. This analyst, classically trained, a German refugee of 65 or so, was famous for reading the Tarot, and singing Schubert lieder concerts in the high school auditorium at night. He was totally out of place in naive, unanalytic America, with all his dark Magic Mountain romanticism, but it seemed to him that here at least, in this childish country, killing had not yet been elevated to a moral imperative, evil was in its springtime. He was seeing a few American students for fifty cents a session, knowing full well that they were in desperate trouble. Dr. Hof knew that Isabel had gotten herself into quite a pickle, what with her miserable marriage and being pregnant now. John said he'd walk Isabel over to Dr. Hof's, he was worried about his weight and he needed the exercise anyway.

"I feel so small," said Isabel, on the walk over to Dr.

Hof's with John. She was already two months pregnant. She slipped her hand into his.

"Like bread and butter," said John. "I used to walk like this with my son."

He had a son and his son was with his divorced wife, Doreen.

"There is a force and it's pushing me into the ground," said Isabel the girlchild.

John laughed and thought she was Emily Dickinson again. "It's because you're pregnant," he said.

He waited for her while she was in there with Dr. Hof, and then they walked on into the hills holding hands. They said more things, like bread and butter and Emily Dickinson, and laughed a few sad, uncomfortable laughs. He was trying to make his living as a cobbler now, working as a fill-in cobbler in different cities bordering their city.

"Armenians have always fixed shoes," he laughed... "I'm one of those sad motherfuckers who goes back to his tradition."

After she had the baby, she ran into him one night at a party. It was a week-night party. She was having her evening of getting out of the house away from the baby. It wasn't a party really, Just a place to go after the bars closed down, somebody said why don't we all go over to my place?

"Remember that crazy Dr. Hof?" he said to her. "You were afraid to go there alone, so I went with you."

"He *was* pretty crazy," she said.

"I think he had the hots for you."

"He was always peeking from behind the curtains. I used to see him peeking from the street below. I think he was masturbating waiting for me."

"So much for mysticism and his rare Tarot deck," said John.

He sat there laughing and sitting like he was stuck to the place, that John, like a statue, a ceramic statue of a bulldog, with a high, white glaze, desperate jowls.

"Can you take me home?" She said to him when Derek the diabetic drunk started talking dirty. She was crying behind her sunglasses, her night out had been one colossal failure.

He took her home like a great-uncle delivering her to her husband. They did not hold hands. Everybody wondered why she was so good, why was she so faithful to her wayward husband. He walked her to her door saying something boring, they had never been able to have one decent conversation despite their affinity.

Then one day she was 38 years old. She was walking

by a large shoe repair store on University Avenue and he, John, was sitting in the window hammering. He looked large, and he flashed a big, good-natured, big-hearted, many-toothed, dispossessed Armenian smile at her. Yes, she still had the husband, and now it was three children. Her poetry had come to nothing and the Emily Dickinson routine was over.

"But where do you live?" she said, "you must live somewhere, you must give me your number."

"Do you really want my number?   What will you do with it?" he squealed.

"Of course I want your number silly, why would I ask you otherwise?   But I'm afraid to come to your house, you know, you've always been provocative for me, John. I'll call you up and we can meet on some neutral grounds... we can go have a coffee or something."

He laughed a perfectly squandered laugh, and flung down his hammer in a pile of leather heel remnants.

"Well, it's true John!" she said.

This made him even more hysterical. He wiped his hands on his medium-blue-gray apron and stood there slapping his sides and howling, surrounded by nails. She waved to him in his window at his cobbler's bench as she went. He was quite bald and the blue apron was the blue of early darkness on a cold rainy day. His hair was mostly steel grey now.

She never called John, like she had promised she would. Then one day her husband took the children snowing for the weekend. She sat in the large empty house in the darkness. It was midnight when she called him.

"Hello John, this is Isabel."

"Isabel?"

"Sure. Don't you know an Isabel? What are you doing right now? Am I disturbing you?"

"You're not disturbing me."

"What were you doing right now?"

"I'm just sitting on my bed. Reading old copies of the *London Economist*."

"Oh, don't let me disturb you."

"How could you disturb me? I'm already disturbed."

"Do you ever do anything like go out for coffee?" she asked, blushing into the phone.

"Sure!" he laughed.

"Would you like to meet me?"

They met. He looked like an old limping hulk coming towards her at the cafe, as she stood in the doorway. waiting and shivering, wearing a very light jacket,... while the hulk, smiling a frayed, inappropriate teddy bear smile, came closer towards her. There was nothing to say as they had coffee. She stirred her cappuccino listlessly and sipped her chocolate flavored froth from her small Italian spoon. She wore a very short mini skirt that was too tight and too short and impossible to walk with. When all the business of the coffee was over with, she asked him to walk her to her car. She could only take very small steps with the tight mini skirt, and she held his hand.

"Can you come home with me? I'm alone and I'm a little afraid. The house seems so empty with the children gone."

"Are you sure?" he said.

"Oh, don't worry, you'll only stay a little while."

When they got home, they went into the livingroom. She threw down her purse on the couch, and threw herself down after it. John sat down too. "Isn't it all strange?" she said, and she hugged him desperately, that frayed teddy bear, wearing a Hawaiian shirt. Then they necked on the couch and he took off the shirt.

"I've lost a few pounds," he said, "does it show?" And he got up and did a little bear dance for her, proud of his figure. She laughed loudly too loud as they kissed and felt each other on the couch and he laughed even louder.

"Don't laugh so loud, the neighbors are excitable," she

said.

Then he laughed even louder. And after many loud laughs, he went home. He said he'd walk across town to where his car was.

Several weeks passed. One day, she called him up again.

"What are you doing today?" she said.

"Just bored," he said.

"Why don't we go somewhere?"

"My car is kaput," he said.

"I'll bring mine," said Isabel. She had an old car.

"Pick me up," he said.

He was waiting for her in front of his house, which was an old house on top of a used bookstore. It was a warm, gorgeous day and all the students were milling around, licking ice cream cones. He looked decrepit and old in his Hawaiian shirt with short sleeves, and his hair was plastered down with water. He gave her the big Armenian smile and the horse laugh.

First they needed gas. Then he said "wait", and he popped out of the car and into a liquor store. He came out with a small bottle of vodka which he put in the back pocket of his beige Levis, an old man with beige Levis, with a small bottle of no-name vodka stuck in his back pocket.

It was a very strange park they drove to in Marin County. Nobody was there that day except a few young couples bicycling, and twelve year old boys on paper routes. They parked her old pale blue Chevrolet and began a walk deep into the park.

"Do you want some?" he asked, holding up the vodka.

She could have used a shot, but she was macrobiotic that day so she said no. On they walked, deeper and deeper into the park, and they found themselves suddenly alone. And then she jumped on him. She jumped on his Hawaiian shirt and hugged his big hairy chest. Then, she unzipped his fly and took out his pecker and kissed that too.

"My god," he said, "I never knew you were so sexy."

She laughed and laughed. Then she got down on all fours like she was a dog.

"Get on my back," she said, "I want to carry you."

"I never *dreamed* you were so sexy!"

"Either did I," said Isabel.

Then they climbed a high rock and he stood on it and peed down into the mud.

"What do you wanna be when you grow up?" she asked.

He laughed and laughed.

"Choo Choo!" he yodeled. "I wanna be a train engineer."

Gradually a thin story about numbers and sentences trickled out of his mouth.

"I've been thinking, take the sentence: "He is good." Now, what does that mean?   Does the 'is' refer to the 'good'... does the 'good' refer to the 'is', and who is 'he'?"

"I don't know," she said. "I don't think about things like that."

"Don't you really?"

"I think about other things," she said.

"What do you think about?   What puzzles you?"

"I don't know," she said.

"Yes," he said, scraping the rock with his finger. "I've been thinking about that a lot lately."

When they emerged from the depths of the park, there was the car, waiting for them where they had left it.

"Has the Chevrolet had an experience while you and I had an experience?" she said.

At this, he laughed. She loved making them laugh. Making them laugh was her specialty. She got into the car and he got in next to her.

"This time you drive," he said.

"What shall we do?" she said.

"Let's eat," he said. "Do you like Mexican food?"

They picked up a hitchhiker who had a harmonica

and a backpack.

"Play us a song," she said.

"I'm just learning," he said.

"Oh, come on. Just anything," said Isabel.

He played them something more charming than if he had really played. On she drove. He sat beside her, and the hitchhiker with the harmonica sat in back. Then they were alone again.

"Do you like Chinese or Italian? Or, do you like Mexican food?" he said.

"I want some fish with hot vegetables," said Isabel. They sat opposite each other in the scratchy booth of an old Chinese restaurant.

"They know me here, they make a special dish for me," said John. While they waited for it to come, he said, "I'm eating with your smell on my hands."

"That's not so terrible," said Isabel.

"Here, smell it," he said. He gave her his hand to smell.

"It's not so bad," she said.

"It's pretty strong," he said.

She began to feel vaguely irritated. After dinner, they drove to his place. She got into bed with him. It was a little cot in a little room with one barren lightbulb on top of everything. He went down on her again and again. Finally, exhausted, her mouth dry, she tiptoed with her bare feet on his linoleum floor to the kitchen sink to get some water. She stood naked at the sink in his dark and the moonlight cast its light on his two prescription medicine bottles standing on the window sill. She felt deeply nauseated. She tried to read the prescriptions to see what they were about but they only said, "John Avakian. Two capsules twice a day for pain." She tiptoed back to bed.

"I just don't understand you women," he said. "Here I've gone down on you again and again and you just haven't shown the slightest interest in doing anything to me."

"I don't feel like doing anything to you," she said.

"You're all so self-centered," he said. "I just don't understand what you want."

"To be self-centered, I guess, is what we want," she said.

They said nothing.

"I need to make a phone call," she said.

"The phone's in there," he said.

He lay on the bed, all crunched up like a paralysis victim. She tiptoed into the other room and phoned, in a whisper, to the Women's History and Research Library, where her friend Ruth lived. If you ever need help, if you're ever in a jam, call, said Ruth, and if I'm not there, leave a message with the answering service. But Ruth wasn't there. The answering service took her message, but what could she say? "Just say Isabel called," she said, and she went back to the little window sill in the kitchen again, and she stood by the sink again, reading the labels on the prescription bottles over and over again, naked in the moonlight. The house was dark with linoleum floors. She liked moving around in it naked, knowing that he was on the bed in the other room. With half a heart she went down on him and when he finally came, she felt so terrible. Then it was time to go home. She put on her things and he walked her to the back door and kissed her. Then she walked away.

She only saw him one more time. She had gone for Sunday breakfast with her friend Shadow and Shadow's two kids, and another woman named Barbara. It was a rowdy group, Shadow's kids whining and crying the whole time. When they got out of the car, there was John, sitting high up on the eighth step of that same gray back porch reading the Sunday paper. He was wearing shorts, cut offs, and those 49 cent Japanese rubber bath thongs. He looked like he had just come out of the bath.

"Let's get outta here, there's somebody I don't wanna see across the street," said Isabel.

"Who?" asked Shadow.

"Just somebody I had a thing with," said Isabel, the no-longer girlchild.

The kids all squawked in the restaurant. Barbara Jones was treating and it was twenty bucks wasted on nothing because nobody could talk, they might just as well have stayed home for breakfast. He was still there on the steps when they got back to the car, he had a way of looking stuck to one place, that John.

"See that guy on the steps over there, reading?" I don't wanna see him," said Isabel.

He looked like he was just idling away any Sunday, all the symbols of contented idleness were there, the cutoffs, the 49 cent bath shoes, the Sunday comics. But there was a line from where Isabel stood that went straight across the street, straight from her nose and through the traffic into a spot between his eyes, and she could see, she could feel, into his very soul. There it was, gray, and desperate, and in flames.

Then one day, was it a few months later? Isabel's husband came home for dinner. She was peeling onions, or washing the breakfast dishes, whatever. Her husband was older now, in a corduroy jacket, the color of melting caramel. Reading the bills, he said,

"...did you hear about John?"

"No, which John?"

"John Avakian."

They had several friends named John. She looked up at him.

There was a pile of white, ripped-open junk mail on the table, mixed in with onion peels.

"John Avakian. He drove his car into a bus on the Freeway. He was killed instantly. He was coming home late at night from some other town after doing a days' work as a cobbler there. They say he was probably drinking, Farrell told me, I ran into Farrell on the way home, I stopped off at the Co-op.

He had no family. Friends took up a collection. His ashes were scattered over the Bay from an airplane. Needless to say, Isabel never saw him again, or her girlchild self either.

* * *

the participant

He was a medium-sized man as he walked down the street in a chocolate brown suit, he had a brown and white striped shirt on, one cuff was dirty. He looked a little out of it to Rosalyn, coming along down the street of *her* bed and breakfast in Amsterdam on her way to the Reik's Museum. She saw him as she waddled along in those white summer clogs she had bought, very hi-heeled white, corked, summer clogs she had already taken a big flop with on the cracked pavement in London. She had bought the clogs to go to Europe with.

She had gone back to her hotel to change into something cooler, and to take her medicine, but as she was changing from out of her navy blue turtle neck woolen sweater, "made expressly for J. Magnin in Hong Kong," she knew she was going to meet a man that day, it was something, just a feeling that she was tired of being alone, tired of being in somber navy blue, her body all wrapped up in woolens. It was twelve o'clock now, time for the noon dose of her medicine. The little French doctor, he had said "pas de risque", this French doctor with the bicycle in his bathtub. She had asked to use the ladies room before going into the examining room, and he had carefully, ever so politely, ushered her into a bathroom, looking more like a little usher at the movies than a doctor. She was surprised to see, of all things, a bicycle in his bathtub, she had never noticed such a quirk in the U.S. before. The doctor quickly apologized, in a French she could hardly understand, and Rosalyn, after a pee, came back into the room for the examination.

Madame Orlovsky stayed with her the whole time in the examining room, translating back and forth from Rosalyn to the doctor, Mme. Orlovsky, who had been swindled out of her husband's estate by the lawyer who had befriended her, she was a constant fixture in the breakfast room of Rosalyn's cheap hotel, attached, as it were, to her own coffee cup and her own small jar of instant coffee.

The small French doctor, growing bald, with the little hips, examined Rosalyn and announced that there was "pas de risque" for her to take the train from Paris to Amsterdam the next day. He wrote her some prescriptions, and that was that.

So here she was in Amsterdam. It was 12 noon. The

sun was out now, and there was a warmth in the air. She had put on a very short yellow dress, really, it was too short to wear alone, so she put her blue jeans on under it, and she knew she was scared and desolate and that she needed somebody to at least take her out to a movie or a restaurant. She applied the soulful plum mascara and the light green creamy eye shadow, she combed out her hair and brushed it, and so on, she did all the things girls know how to do to hide their utter desolation. The truth was her skin looked green from being inside, what with these stomach pains she had had, she had spent many hours on her bed in that no-star hotel in Paris. She rubbed a lot of Amber Soleil #4 , orange gelée, into her face, and voila! though she still felt sick to her stomach, she looked like she had a tan, and she headed for the Museum. (She had so longed to go to Greece, to the Greek Islands, where you could live for $2 a day and have Everything, water, the sun, music, ouzo, the warm Greek people, what was she doing here?)

"You look like a tourist also," she said to the ordinary-looking, medium-sized man in the chocolate brown suit. "I can tell, because you're walking along looking at buildings.

The man only smiled.

"I'm on my way to the Reik's Museum," she said "I have a date with a friend."

The man smiled again. "Yes?" he said.

"Yes," said Rosalyn, "do you happen to know the time? we're supposed to meet at 2"

She couldn't tell if the man was listening to her, but she went on talking nervously anyway, as if to say, don't hurt me, please. See? I can walk, I can talk, I can say interesting things.

"I don't even know if she'll show up. We made this date on a lark, six weeks ago. We ran into each other in London, and she said she'd be in Amsterdam on August 30th to catch her plane home, and I said I had to catch mine from Amsterdam also, on September first, so we made this appointment, how you say..."rendezvous?"

The man in the chocolate brown suit, looking a little like a wolf, smiled.

"Gunnar is my name," he said.

She hadn't met many women on this trip. There were very few women her age traveling abroad alone. Younger women, yes, you saw them eating their petit déjeuner, breaking French bread, eating it with lots of confiture. You saw them eating breakfast, just back from Nice or Cannes, or a Greek Island, you saw them in the breakfast room

In Berkeley's Green and Pleasant Land   36

with their slender boyfriends, in jeans, all wearing jeans, all eating confiture, all brown and slender and naked-looking, fresh from Cannes or Nice. But there were few women her age. She had met that one woman on the London Tube, the woman, sitting down, studying her Tube map, obviously a tourist, obviously American, obviously scared.

"Hello," said Rosalyn," I bet you're American. How long have you been traveling?"

"Not long," said the woman, "I've been here four days and I'm going home."

"But why?" asked Rosalyn, knowing all along. "Do you have any children?"

"Two," said the woman.

"I have four," said Rosalyn.

"I arranged it all so my ex-husband would be with them this summer," the woman said.

"Me too. We have a lot in common," said Rosalyn, "Maybe we should be traveling together. Are you Jewish?"

"Yes," the woman sighed.

"We really *should* be traveling together," said Rosalyn.

"I can't. I'm going home tomorrow. It's done. I even called up my ex-husband last night, and I had to be pretty desperate to do that. 3000 miles away, divorced two years ago, and I'm calling him to ask what I should do. This is my stop, how many monuments and museums can I shlep myself to?" And she was gone, out the door forever.

So the man's name was Gunnar, as if it mattered.

"I'm American," said Rosalyn, from California, Berkeley."

"You didn't have to tell me that," he said, laughing. He had green teeth and green eyes and hair like straw. Rosalyn looked at him and said, still keeping up the "don't hurt me, I'm interesting" game, "You look vaguely like that Swedish actor that plays the so-called Christ figure in Ingmar Bergman'a movies "

"Oh no. Not me," he said. He wore beige suede shoes, gum-soled, the shoes of a foreigner.

"I don't even know if my friend will show up, her name is Alice, we're both into the women's movement, I don't suppose you know what that is?"

"What?" said Gunnar, in his best crippled English.

"Well, you have heard of women?" said Rosalyn.

"Vomen. Yes vomen. Nu, shure," he said.

"Well women. In America, there's a regular revolution."

"Yes?" he said.

"Oh, forget it," said Rosalyn. "My friend wants to see

Kandinsky's wife's paintings, you know? Mme. Kandinsky? *He* is a painter, but she, she is really the painter's painter, you know???"

"I have been in Amsterdam already three weeks," said the man.

Rosalyn was his height with the clogs on, and she walked along with her legs all summery, she had shaved them all the night before, her two legs, and the sun falling on her yellow dress and on her green green eyes with the green eye shadow and the soulful plum mascara. Gunnar said he had a car in a garage, a Jaguar 38 or something. Rosalyn listened. He had a car. He had been all over. There were lovelier places than Amsterdam in Holland, he could take her to all of them, he had been to these places, you needed a car to get there. He had also been to Greece, to Spain, to Portugal, Italy, you name it, he had been there and everywhere.

"But, don't you work?" asked Rosalyn.

"My time is my own now. I am very advanced in, how you say? the advanced mathematick. Very advanced in my field, how you say? Computer? I go back to Stockholm when I be ready, when I be all traveled out," he said, laughing.

He took her all over. She didn't want to leave

Amsterdam with him because she was afraid of him. After all, she didn't know him, but he took her all over in Amsterdam. First, he took her to sit down in the sun and have one of those afternoon drinks they all have in Europe, sitting in the sunshine. He leaned forward and kissed her on the lips, and then he leaned back, and she sat watching him smile at her through the sunlight, and then she noticed that he had a crippled hand. One hand just, one hand was crippled, and he hid it in his brown suit, he hardly ever stuck it out. He had such a strong other hand. It was as strong as two hands. She saw it while he sat drinking his gin and tonic in the bright afternoon sunshine as she sat facing him, watching him drink. He leaned forward again, and he touched her hand, and he said, "sweet kind, ich liebe dich, sweet baby," and she smiled politely now, and he saw that she saw about his hand, so he smiled again. "Adorable little girl," he said, "would you like another drink? Here, taste mine," and she tasted his drink, and it wasn't half-bad, and, blinking at him through the sunlight, she felt how green her eyes must look right now, how yellow was her dress, and she could tell he wanted another smile from her, so, yes, although it made her eyes tear to do it, and he took her hand, and he touched it, he pressed it, he kissed it, very gently and very smoothly, and she said, this man doesn't love me, he loves my hand! I have two beautiful, two perfect hands, I am a perfectly formed creature, a mermaid perhaps, and he stroked both her hands now, and her eyes teared again, and she felt embarrassed for him now, but glad that he was maimed, and there were two young theater-revolutionaries sitting near them, leaning back in their chairs, and another crippled man played a silly song on his mandolin, a silly refrain, and all the regulars knew it, something like "bobolink! bobolink!" A fairy tale was starting, of that there could be no doubt. She did not adore the prince of this fairy tale, she hardly knew him, this make-do prince, he was the prince 's crippled brother anyway, but it was a fairy tale, and she was the main event.

They went all over together. She was not put off by the hand, she felt a loyalty to it actually, as though she had finally met the old friend she was destined for. He always stood on that side of her so his good hand could hold her around. They seemed to go round together, in circles, reeling, reeling and rolling through streets and squares, disaffected mannequins, they'd come to Rembrandt's statue in the center of the square, stand and gape, and reel again. They reeled around and gaped wherever they went, they reeled and gaped at trinkets in windows, at pictures of naked girls in the glass cases outside nightclubs, they reeled and gaped everywhere, at anything. Finally, it was suppertime, and Gunnar said, "We eat, huh?" triumphant as Balboa discovering the Pacific. He took her to a restaurant where he knew the maitre d'.

"I don't know what to order," said Rosalyn, "my stomach..."

The maitre d' came over and promised he would give her the best for her stomach.

"Let him do it, he knows," said Gunnar.

They ate and drank, and when they were through with dinner, they left the restaurant to reel through the streets some more. There was not that much to look at after Mme. Tussaud's... so they were forced to gape at some more nudie-cutie pictures in the glass showcases outside the nightclubs.

"I like that one," said Rosalyn, trying to add some interest to the evening. She pressed her nose up against the glass and pointed to a dark-haired woman vomiting up two huge silicon breasts in her face.

"No, she is too sexy," Gunnar said, "she is too much already."

"Then how about that one? said Rosalyn, pointing to a more demure, quiet-featured, refined type. "What do you think of her?"

"I like yours, I want to see yours," said Gunnar.

Then they reeled some more. They reeled to coffee bars and piano bars, and one cognac and coffee after another. Suddenly it was 4 a.m.

"I not want sleep alone tonight," said the man,

She didn't really want to sleep with him. For one thing, she didn't know him, he might be crazy.

"I can't sleep with you," she said. "You might be crazy, you might hurt me."

"Oh no, I never. I brootale never, to any woman. I not brootale. I am not strong. I cannot hurt you. You see, you are stronger than me."

"I'll see you in the morning," she said, "then we can start our day, we can do it tomorrow after I know you a little better."

"Look, you do not trust me. We have been together all evening, and still you do not trust."

"No, I do not trust," she said.

"I feel sad for you. Something must have happened to you in your life."

"Yes?" she said.

"Somebody must brootale to you," he said.

In the background, a hippie offered his dog a large

pan of water, from a fountain.

"Come with me," he pleaded. "I gentle to you be, I love you. I love you, come."

"I need some presents for my kids," she said.

"The nice Dutch dresses. Come. We go to sleep now and tomorrow in the morning, we go to buy the nice Dutch dresses, on . . . Strasse."

"Are you sure?" she said.

"Come. In the morning we wake up together. We get an early start. First we go buy the nice Dutch dresses for the children. Then to Ann Frank's house. Then it is already lunchtime, so we have a little lunch, and then to Rembrandt's house. A canal ride. A movie maybe. And then I take you to airport where you get your plane home."

"You mean it? You'll come with me to Ann Frank's house?"

"With you I go anywhere," he said sadly. Come, we sleep together."

But she didn't want to. Back and forth they argued. Finally, he spat the cigarette out of his mouth and cursed his life.

"It's not you, don't take it personally," she said.

"I sorry for you because you do not trust."

"Right, I do not trust."

"Somebody has been brootale to you," he said.

"Yes," she said, somebody, everybody, the world.

"I sorry for you, somebody. Somebody come and ruin your life."

"Take me to my hotel," she said.

"Yes, yes, we going now."

"Please, let me think about it a little more," she said. walking after him sullenly.

He led the way. Finally, he stopped in front of a hole in the wall.

"Look, this here is nice hotel. See? They take American Express here, all your credit cards."

"But I don't want to be locked in a room with you."

He laughed.

"The clerk stays up 24 hours a night here, you will not be alone," he said.

"Are you sure? How do you know?" she said.

"I promise I gentle to you be. I not. Brootale no, brootale never."

"All right then, if you're sure," she says.

"Come, we go to sleep now. I no want alone tonight."

"I have no birth control," she mutters.

He runs down the street, an ordinary, medium-sized figure. She puts her bag down, leans against the building, the sky dark and foreign. Finally, he returns, breathless.

"Everything's closed," he says, "I couldn't get anything."

They go into the hotel. The man shows them the room. It is a nice room and he is a nice enough man. It has a good-looking bathtub with tile and lots of hot water. The man wears blue cotton pajamas and has his finger stuck in a pocketbook on the page he is reading. He never looks at Rosalyn, Gunnar does all the business with him.

"I don't know," says Rosalyn, "does he really stay up the whole night?"

"She wants to know if you are up all night, she needs someone up the whole night," he says.

The man says he reads and then he goes to sleep, and he is up making early breakfast in the morning.

"Tell him I need somebody up all night," she says.

"She needs to have... what? Up all night? Ach! I can't talk with her! I don't understand these Americanische!"

"Tell him I'm afraid. Tell him I don't know you and this is the first time we're together in a hotel room, go ahead, tell him."

"She is afraid, the Americanische. She takes her plane back to America tomorrow and she is nervous."

The man in the pajamas laughs. "I no understand her.

In Berkeley's Green and Pleasant Land   46

She crazy!" he says.

"She just afraid," says Gunnar.

"I sleep. Of course I sleep! I read in the kitchen and then I sleep. And then I wake up and . . . I make breakfast."

"Yes, well, sure," says Gunnar.

"What does she think I do? Crazy American cunts! Need a good screw!"

"Well, should we take it?" says Gunnar.

"I don't know," she says.

"Decide. It's 75 guilders."

"All I want to do is sleep," says Rosalyn.

"Yes, we take," says Gunnar to the man in the blue pajamas.

They take the elevator upstairs.

He lay on the bed waiting, the little mashed-up hand beside him, in a state of quiet. She goes into the bathroom. It is a good bathroom, because the room costs 75 guilders. There is tile on the floor, a good bathtub, a steady, thick outpouring of hot water, and the toilet works. She creams her face, and lays out all her cosmetics from the Gladbag, which is dirty now, there is a hole in it, and the little red Maybelline eyebrow pencil falls out of the hole into the sink. Toothpaste has smeared the inside of the

Gladbag and it hangs over the glass shelf under the bathroom mirror, all besmirched like a defeated bladder. She cleans her face with the strawberry yogurt organic cleansing cream, and puts on the perfume George has given her, Je Reviens, but she hopes George will never return, it wasn't that easy to get rid of him. Rubbing lipstick into her cheeks, like a slave girl I look, with coins on my hips, she says to the sorry face in the mirror there.

And what of him?

She thinks, some man . . . on a bed all stretched out and waiting . . . they all look the same, pink and helpless, and a little crippled, and their thing like so many pink worms rolled into one, magnified. She comes into the room (not quite the way she wants, but the man, he is no beauty either), frightened, despairing, and all perfumed, holding her clothes out in a little bundle in front of her, wearing the clogs to look taller and leggier and sexier, he looks ridiculous under the clean hotel sheets, with the silly grin on his face, she, having thrown her clothes on a chair, jumps into bed with him, you needed a body to commit this crime, he: Mr. State-Your-Name / Have-You-Ever-Been-Charged-With-a-Felony-or-a-Misdemeanor? / Your-Age-and Social-Security Number?/ reaching for her disenchanted labia, tries to insert his worm.

"No you don't! Asshole!" she yells.

"La Nature," he had said, standing in front of the Reik's Museum, just a few hours before, he meant this, licking pussy and sticking it in after jabbing his cock up your ass, without even washing it.

"My God! Where's your hygiene?" she yells, "wash it off before you do that!"

And he jumps off the bed, a little self-satisfied gnome, with one hand missing, it has just a thumb, that poor hand, the rest of it a solid lump, no fingers, she is sad for all the men she has known, all with that crippled thing between their legs, and the way they pretend it's so gorgeous. He is positively whistling in there while the water runs and she can see something pink messing around with water, the fool, doesn't he know?

"Your skin is dry, where's the suntan oil?" he says, and he rubs Bain de Soleil #4 onto her legs and the backs of her legs, executing a muff dive, and, for the hundredth time . . . or the millionth, she starts her sad girl ritual, whoever told her you had to give every man a blow job . . . it is a million worms, and it carries her off to wormland where they live, and he jumps off the bed again, runs into the bathroom again, and the water is on full force again, and he shouts through the water in the bathroom, "I didn't do anything, I held back, I'm putting it under cold water right now, a doctor showed me how, you hold back, and then you put cold water on it from the faucet, and then you can come."

"You goddamned liar!" she says, "I have my hand up there right now and I can smell all the sperm that is up inside me!"

"Yes, yes," he says, in a phenomenal glee.

"Smell this finger," she says.

"That's you," he says. "Look, what's the big problem? What's worst can happen to you? You can have nice baby boy. You have nice baby boy and in nine months I come to California and marry you."

"I don't want baby boy!"

"What you got against baby boys?"

"I told you, I have enough."

"You not want marry me?"

"I don't want to sweep your floors and I don't want to do your laundry," she says.

"Don't worry, we have it nice. In Sweden, there is no poor, I make lot of money. We have nice summer house and winter house and nice baby boy, and we go on vacations. We have nice car, Volvo."

"No," she cries, "No. I don't want to be married, I

don't know who you are, get off me before I call the hotel manager."

"You call the hotel manager?!" And the man laughs and laughs. "The hotel manager is down there washing his own dick in cold water, or else, he's reading mystery in kitchen in his pajamas."

"Oh," she groaned. And she thought of her sweet children back home, and her estranged, jerky, husband, and oh, her children, her children, her poor innocent children. She knew that the man had promised not to come in her, and she had believed him, like the jerk she was, and she knew now that her whole tract or whatever you called it, was full of sperm now, no matter what she did, but she lay in the tub sadly, anyway, not knowing whether she was driving the sperm up even farther, or pushing them out, that's what happens when you fuck with strangers, something said.

"Why don't you call down and say we want breakfast sent up?" said the man.

She picks up the receiver, and calls down.

"They're bringing it up," she says, turning to him, he is sleeping now, the little stump of a hand resting under his chin like a baby.

Marry him? That stupid ass! Marry that fool? I don't

want to have his baby, It'll probably have a stump like him.

"The breakfast is coming, wake up, wake up, Gunnar," she says.

He smiles a dumb smile.

"Ich liebe dich," he says, "I love you, we have baby boy and get married."

She was stuck with a fucking stump-handed baby.

"Knock, knock. One coffee, one tea," says the maid.

He sat cross-legged, naked on a chair, the tray on a table between them. She had the dress on, the yellow dress with the summery grass blowing in the print of it, the summery grass on a summery day, and her cunt all wet with the sperm of a stump-handed baby. She wore no pants. She just sat there with her dress on, it was very short, her legs were crossed, and her hairy snatch showed, she knew that, and she carefully picked up a piece of ham between two fingers, and then she buttered her roll with that good sweet Amsterdam butter and the cheese, and he, sitting naked and satisfied, with his balls pressed between his legs, drinking the coffee and eating the ham and cheese, and it was very intimate somehow, and she knew that at least she was having this intimate scene with somebody, and the hair between her legs, and her thighs all like that, and that he could look right up into her snatch as he ate his ham and she ate hers, and she said, "I like this breakfast, I like these breakfasts of cheese and ham and butter and rolls they serve in Amsterdam. They're a welcome relief after the breakfasts in Paris," and he doesn't bother answering her, nor does he bother to hide his crippled hand anymore, and they sit there eating it all and she can feel the come dripping from between her legs into the hotel-upholstered chair.

"They called up before when you were sleeping, a girl is coming up to clean the room by 11, we have to hurry and get out of here."

Gunnar gets dressed and so does Rosalyn. She sits in the bathroom slicing the little glass bottles that the French doctor has given her, two little bottles emptied into half a glass of water.

He is a stranger to her now in his brown suit as they go carry her bag to Left Luggage at the station, the cuff of his shirt is really filthy. They go get a drink, she needs a glass of water or soda to pour the little vials of medicine into, it is time for her midday dose.

Upstairs, she sits down in a very old room, and he orders an orange soda for her.

"I'll be right back," he says, " I have to go use the toilet."

She is sitting. The room is very old. It is something out of the Thirties, all the doors and even the waiter and the soda bottles, they are from the Thirties too. She sits there in the ugly room. It is like a dream, this room in an old railroad station where they serve you an orange drink, and the waiters match the room, and she starts sawing off the tip of one of the little glass bottles to pour into the orange drink. Her table is right near the door and she is watching the people come and go, so many men with brown suits. They all come into the room, some only wearing brown jackets or brown pants, but brown is everywhere, ubiquitous brown, men in brown suits, and it all matches the chairs, and the mustard-color walls, walls in her dreams, walls of the Thirties, walls of the halls of apartment buildings, and elevators, and movies, and her elementary school, and it all matches the dirty brown orange soda, she, in her short dress featuring wildflowers in the sunlight, it is too short, really, up to her snatch in fact, and certain creepy men say "hello, girlie," displaying broken teeth, slicing, sitting, the dress frankly pornographic, odd shaped medicine bottles, men, coming and going, in and out, brown.

The waiter comes to ask will the gentleman pay, and she says yes, he'll be here soon, but Gunnar is taking very long to come back. "Pardon me," she says to another man in brown, "can you see if a man is in there in the WC, he's wearing a brown suit." "Nobody's there," says the stranger, coming back, "except one guy, to check up on him."

Her plane out of Amsterdam doesn't leave till 6 the next morning. She will spend the day, at the Reik's Museum, thank God for museums, whoever realized their true value? She walks out of Central Station into the sunny day, and catches the #2 bus to the Reik's museum. Thank God for the #2 bus, and for Mme. Kandinsky, she's alive, who knows, he might have killed her, she gets off easy with a cunt full of bad genes sperm. Soon it will be all over, the sad, solitary business of the sad, solitary female, endangered, bereft, transforming experience into disgust. Soon, she'll board the plane and the stewardesses will be in charge of reality for a change. Her estranged husband will meet her at the airport with her children. She is dying to see them, "it will be the happiest moment of my life" she has written to him, "to see them at the airport." (What had she done on this trip, what really? Her philandering husband had convinced her to go away for a vacation, "go to Europe," he said, "get away from the kids." It had seemed fair, he had gone, according to their separate arrangements, the summer before, "Have some time away, taste your own experience, savor, savor." True, her body was all riveted with mafia bullets, running to take care of their every need, the running never stopped. But what had she done when she got to her Valhalla, what was there to do when you fled from the children, take busses to museums? Pick up men? One of the first things she had done when she got to London was buy her girlies English underwear in a London department store, panties with the Union Jack girlishly emblazoned on the hip, red, white, and blue, indeed, what had she done when she got to Amsterdam, but buy them the authentic wooden shoes for walking on the Zuider Zee, four pairs, one for each child, how was she ever going to fit them into her bag for the plane ride home? Children once you had them, there was no getting away, it was a phony myth, if they weren't with you, they were deep, deep, in your sub-cortex, without them, it was all cold, tasteless, trivial, sad.)

She boards the #2 bus. "Wait, Mme. Kandinsky, wait! I'm gonna hang with you all afternoon!"

The estranged cheater-husband is there in San Francisco when she lands, the gorgeous children with new haircuts and new clothes. "It is the happiest moment of my life," she whispers to no one. "I thought I'd never see them again." The husband, with affect zero, clitoris smear on his cheek.

After two weeks, Rosalyn can't remember a thing about her trip, maybe a few crude, trashy intimacies. She had heard a joke once about Frank Sinatra. Sinatra is in Las Vegas, he rings Room Service, and says, "Send up anyone." But how can such a joke reveal the essence of her experience, when being alone was terminal, incurable, and anyway, staring down Walnut and Vine Street, with her strong cup of Peet's Decaf French, thawing out, what is her experience, what trajectory called to her, numinous, opulent, through the dark velvet drapes, why such an exorbitant price to be . . . a participant . . . in an event? Dimly, as in a Rorschach blot, she recalled blowjobs on the roof, the ones she had given to strangers, the ones she had given to special friends, and the ones she gave to nobody in particular.

* * *

make haste, my beloved

So at 2:30 in the morning she climbed out of her warm bedclothes and got into the car. Catch the excitement, says the voice. And she rode rode drove drove drizzled fizzled carrizled away. Away, away, left turn, right turn, blinkers where? Catch the excitement says the voice. Left the house that was a cage, only a filthy cage to her. Must the bird clean its own cage? She had heard the Yoga Acting Company was rehearsing Who's Afraid of? Who's Afraid of Who? Who's Afraid of What? Virginia Woolf? Let's face it, who'd be afraid of Virginia Woolf?? She got there just as the group was packing up for the night. She knew the man, his name was Ed.

"What's been doing with you?" said this Ed.

"Nothing new," she said.

"What's old?"

"Not too much there either."

They drove along in his bus.

"You're still in this bus of yours, aren't you?" she said.

"Are we in Mexico or on College Avenue?"

"We're in both," he said.

"I've been going through something," she said.

"What's that?" he said, not being able to look at her while she talked.

Yes, he could not look at her, he could not look. He could not look because it was a homemade bus. Made from an old breadtruck. There were no discernible furnishings in it except a roll of yellow paper towels. Thank you, she wanted to say, thank you.

"I've been going through something," she said, staring out the window as he stared straight ahead out of his, "I've been on the death-rebirth trip."

"Death, rebirth," he said, repeating.

"Yes, death, rebirth."

"How is that different from what you're always on?"

"I can't answer questions," she said.

"Who killed you?" he said.

"I don't know.... all I know is I died."

"Well, let's hope you get reborn," he said.

"Yeh," she said, "yes."

"Here we are," he said, "here we are. This is Bufano's, this is the place."

In they went, to the place.

She sat down. It was a long table. The actors seated themselves. At the far end a woman with a red flowing shirt and gray tinted glasses, through the glasses a pair of Velasquez eyes. A small man next to her swore he was her husband. Opposite sat Fay, Fay the director, Fay who had been thru it all with her four marriages, her four teenagers, one whoring in Oakland, one in a jail in Anchorage Alaska, Fay who had left her clerical job in the radical law offices to open her acting school. Around the table it went. People. People. People around the table sat. And at other tables, other people. A wife of a biology professor who had lately discovered her "amazon qualities," out with an exceptionally short chubby man with a cherub's face. Paying, ordering. Drinking, talking. Through darkness, through candle flames.

"The mob, it's the mob," Fay was saying. "I watched *Long Day's Journey* on TV last night and it was good but it doesn't come thru on TV."

"No, it doesn't come thru, it doesn't come thru."

"The only thing I have against expressionist sets is the angles. I'm tired of that sharp line. Now, if we could use plastic. Plastic you can bend."

"I know what you mean about *Long Day's Journey*, I know what you mean."

"It's the stage, man, the stage adds another dimension."

"It's not that mystical," said the woman somehow. Mystical, shmystical, she was beginning to use the words again. The words. I have to look up Shakespeare tonight when I get home, she thought. Where is that little line, "rounded by a little sleep"?

"It's only the people."

"It's only the mob."

"It's the ritual."

"Yes, the ritual."

"And the ritual!"

"And a mob."

"And a ritual."

"It's only a ritual!"

"Pity and fear."

"Terror and fear."

"Kierkegaard and Carlos Castenada."

"Pity and fear, fear and terror."

"What are you afraid of? Death is stalking you."

"Over your left shoulder."

"Fear and trembling Kierkegeard."

"I have noticed," the woman was saying now. She had noticed, she had noticed what? What after all *had* she noticed? She had noticed absolutely nothing these 41 years, absolutely nothing. But what had the others noticed? What had any of them noticed? The little athletic molecular biologist she had fucked in his room at the Shattuck Hotel, what had he noticed, and he was a Nobel Prize winner practically, nobody's dummy, was he? "Isn't this good," he said, "isn't this what it's all about," he said, plunging into her, "yes, yes," she said, thank you, yes, she could hardly speak with his weight on her. "Yes, yes, thank you," "isn't this nice," he said, "can you think of anything nicer you'd rather be doing, isn't this the nicest time?" he said. "Yes, yes," she said, "yes, it's like running five miles," he said, "it's as good as running five miles," "thank you yes," she said she felt glad, that he could rid himself of having to run the five miles for that day, thank you, to help him go through this one day with one less obsession, liberate! "Liberate all sentient beings," chanted the Buddhists, and wouldn't you know it, she cried. You are now entering Chakra City, population Eternity, said the sign, 'Liberate All Sentient Beings! Liberate All Sentient Beings spelled the bartender's teeth on fire in Bufano's Cafe. Suddenly a courtroom . . . "I do not notice anything," she said, meekly, in the courtroom of the athletic molecular biologists, "here I am in my brand new Adidas tennis shoes and my new white tennis outfit, and I tell you, you athletic molecular biologist men, I tell you, *I have noticed nothing.*"

"Liberate all sentient beings," cry the Buddhists, storming the courtroom. Eisenstein is holding a stick over their heads to show them the mood, "liberate all sentient beings," they cry in Spanish, running. The molecular biologists all fart and faint at once in a superb Martha Graham choreography.

But there was Fay saying something else now. There was Fay in her yellow sweater. How finely made she was, what beautiful hands coming out of that yellow sweater, what thoroughly Botticelli hands.

"Even at a football game, it's another thing being there, or watching it on TV. . ."

"Yes, yes, the mob, it's the mob," said the woman.

"In Marakesh, did they smoke much dope in Marakesh?"

"It was a scene, man, it was a scene. Little guys hammering out trays right in front of you. Women shaking behind shawls, shifty eyes."

"Yes, yes, it's the football game. It is the football. It is the game. It is Eugene O'Neill."

"Let's face it, he's the best playwright we have."

"Really?" Really thought the woman. But how come I didn't pick him for my Masters Oral? Eugene, Eugene? Where are you? And there she was in the forest with the brambles scratching her knees searching for Eugene again. A child, Eugene is a child now. Children. Eugene? Eugene! Come out! Come out, come out, wherever you are!

I am dying, she thought, I am dying. Please god, please don't let me die. Tonight when I go home I'll pray. No, there won't be time to pray, there won't be time. I better pray right now. I better pray right here in Bufano's.

That's why I need a naturalist set to start out with. When they come in, we want it to look like ordinary people.

"O, my stomach. My stomach. Don't let me die. Please don't let me die . . . May I use your napkin please??"

He looked at her like she was crazy. They had all come into the restaurant together, they had all started out equal, they all got a napkin when they started out, why must she ask for his?

"It's because my tea spilled," she said. "The tablecloth is wet under my elbow. I just want to lean my elbow on some dry paper."

Dry paper? Did I hear myself say, "dry paper"?

"Yes yes," he said. "Take it," but he hated her, she was

a stranger, an intruder, he was an actor, a man. Loose jointed, shit-kicking, he had kicked the shit in Mexico, he had kicked the shit in Marakesh, he had shit under his fingernails, and shit crunched and dried into the rubber heel of his boot. But your type is going out of style now, yes, he had perfected that shit-kicking look, loose, loose, the loose, leathery-faced, I-don't-give-a-fuck-actor, he was telling about working as a stunt man now, riding thru a wall of fire, spread-eagled in a Plymouth. O you spread-eagled type, your type is finished now, they're not casting your type anymore. And then as a gravedigger, Honey worked as a waitress while I was working as a gravedigger, always trying to impress, he was trying to impress now, impress Ed, and Honey, Honey....

"thru flames he rode"

"I passed thru a wall of flames," he said.

A wall of flames yes, thank you yes, thank you all for this wall of flames she said, thank you for this evening, she said . . . thank you I will remember you always, . . . I will hate you forever, thanks, thanks for the memory. I will go home now, I will get back into my nightie now, and I will sleep the sleep of unfulfilled women thank you. Whatever's left of the night I will sleep it, how can I thank you all?

"Wait, I'll drive you to your car," said Ed.

In his bus again, she stared out of her side of the window while he stared out of his, grimly observant of those surreal nighttime streets.

"Gettin' any lately?" he said.

"Not too much very occasionally," she said.

"Slim pickins," he said.

"Yes," she said.

"Slim pickins here for you in Chakra City."

"Liberate!" they said. "Liberate!" cried the Buddhists, "Liberate All Sentient Beings!"

"Tell me something," he said, "do you lady writers masturbate a lot?"

"A lot?" she said.

"Well, let's put it this way, do you masturbate period?"

"What can I say?" she said, "it comes in cycles. I masturbate a lot and then I go for long periods without masturbating at all. But I wouldn't describe myself as a heavy masturbator."

"What would you describe yourself as?"

"A wall of fire," she said.

"You're sure you're not a wall of shit?"

"I'm sure," she said. What good to tell them that you weren't sure?

"I told you that I've just gone thru a death-rebirth experience," she said.

"Lottsa luck," he said.

"Here's your car," he said.

"So, goodnight," she said. And she stepped out of his homemade bus with as much fear and trembling as anybody, into the homemade darkness.

* * *

*at 15,
he had been
a leader in*

Kachka, the Jewish wife in Berkeley from NY, was somehow very restless with her father-in-law visiting from New York this summer. For one thing, she and Lou had just about had it (the terrible marriage) and she was too ashamed for anyone to see it up close. All morning long, Grandpa Max had been out there in the tiny, overgrown backyard hacking away at the thick jungle of blackberry bushes. They had grown to a height of four or five feet and had entirely suffocated the pathway so that nobody could even get back there. Also, the fly of Grandpa Max's pajamas was becoming more and more of a problem, it opened and closed, depending on whether he was swinging forward or back with his machete, the broken-off end of a broom-handle. Really, it was a bit much.

The son had a job teaching summer school in San Francisco that ended at noon. He had gone off to work this morning with the intent of returning home right after work so that he could take his father gambling in Reno. Kachka was frankly tired of Grandpa Max's visit. Many times when she was fed up, she would ask Grandpa Max would he mind if she ran down to the store for a minute to go get fruit or milk. He loved these fruits of California, he had never seen such enormous peaches or cherries or nectarines in the Bronx, he had never even seen an avocado or a papaya before. The only bad thing about these short sprints to the supermarket was that Kachka had to come back home again. Occasionally, she buoyed up her courage with a decaf cappuccino, but for the most part, she rushed right home. Thank God Grandpa Max's stay was coming to an end, not a moment too soon. He had bought a 30 day pass from TWA, and the thirty days was drawing to a close, and he was leaving.

His son Lou had tried showing him a good time in California, taking him everywhere, educating him to the wonders of the California lifestyle. He had even gotten Grandpa Max a date with a sexy woman that he, the son, had just finished an affair with, if you can believe that. Imagine a 65 year old depressed Grandpa Max with a young sexy woman, narcissist-nympho to the bargain, but that was Berkeley for you, "that's what they do here, Poppa!"

she had heard the son insist to the disbelieving father. Kachka had heard her husband setting up the date for Grandpa, she just couldn't believe all this was happening, and right in front of her too, but apparently, she, the Jewish wife in Berkeley from New York, hadn't gotten used to the Berkeley lifestyle either, with its very, peculiar odyssey of self-actualization, free pussy, and human potential rhetoric. Armed with his GI Bill, she and Lou had left New York some years before, happy to escape from the claustrophobic family with its intrusive rules and regulations, to study literature at UC Berkeley. Once a nice Jewish boy from City College, he had gone ape chasing shiksas . . . first as a Pfc. Infantryman . . . in Berlin during the Korean War, then, as a graduate student in English at Berkeley, and now, as citizen-at-large. How innocent he had been once, how deeply excited by the world of ideas, how he had loved Hans Kohn's Intellectual History classes at City College! . . . "Spain contributed three things to Austria during the Thirty Years' War: horses, court manners, and the baroque!", he could imitate Kohn perfectly down to the last umlaut. How it had all changed for Kachka, Jewish wife from New York, nice Jewish boys, a dying breed.

Grandpa Max had appeared at his date's door with a

box of good chocolates, and a bottle of Korbel brandy, a carryover from the son's whoring army days, his strategy . . . for setting up a sexually receptive situation for his old Jewish father. Grandpa Max sat around their rear cottage, smoking his aromatic pipe in his torn pajamas, brought straight from the slum apartment in the Bronx, all the way to sunny California. Lou! his most successful child, married, the father of two pretty little girls. Respectability! Success! Women! How to get them, how to handle them, how to drop them when the time came. They sat around freely discussing this, while Kachka hovered, attending to the children. She was 35 and in the middle of an identity crisis. Each Friday, at half past nine, she went to her sliding-scale psychiatric social worker to discuss her crisis. Imagine, procuring for your father! Imagine, her husband having affairs and even boasting about them to Grandpa Max! In her presence! While she, the un-entertained ghost, muddled around, changing diapers, making lunch. With the help of her social worker, Kachka had figured out that her husband was 'insecure', 'had a problem with intimacy', 'lacked the ego to individuate from his father', overly identifying with him and the depression that had ruined his life, with his impotence, his sixty-five years of sexual deprivation, all of it, but what could Kachka do with all this "insight"? Nothing.

Poor Max. Tumbling he had come, out of a strong matriarchy, like they all did. Cherry Street. The grocery store where all the family shlepped. Dragged out of the 8th grade, sent to work, married, he had married above his class, but she was, after all, a greenhorn, though she was far more accomplished than Max was, the family was opposed to Sara. She had been living in an apartment with her sister Bela on the lower East side, the parents, too immobilized, had stayed on in the old country, but very soon, Bela started taking secret epsom salts enemas, she was too fat for America, her appendix burst, and that was it, she never even called the doctor, too scared, too much the frightened immigrant, leaving the younger sister Sara alone, stranger in a strange land, to marry Max, to bear his children, to suffer with him through the depression, to remember the five or so words from the five or so languages she had learned as a middle-class girl in Romania, three lines of a surrealist poem, and the one piece she played (still) on the piano, a moody Chopin nocturne. They had met coming out of the movies. She had taken him home to her sister's house, there, she played him her one étude. Then, when he lifted his arm to wipe off his face, grimy with poverty and odyssey-less-ness, she said, "Max, your sleeve is torn, give me your jacket, I'll sew it for you."

She fixed his sleeve and they got married. Only to have monstrous children, all branded with problems of depression, impotence, sexual deprivation, promiscuity.

Grandpa Max, tired from his blackberry-machete episode, was now inside the house, sitting in a chair, puffing on his pipe, waiting for his son Lou to come home. Lou was probably picking up his friend Rick Johnson, a California goy, who was to accompany them to Reno, Rick always with new gambling schemes, had taught Lou gambling and whoring and Come/Don't Come at the craps tables. Kachka was feeding the children their lunch, a can of cream of asparagus soup for her two little girls.

"Eat your lunch, Serena, your schoolbus is coming," but the child instead was in the middle of a Batman game with a reluctant Grandpa, "I'll be Cat Woman, you be Falseface, no, you be in trouble, and I'll be Batman, Annabelle, you be Robin, okay Grandpa, now be in trouble."

"Trouble?" said Grandpa Max. Sara, his wife of 41 years had died two years ago, he had a few months before retired from a nonskilled factory job in the Bronx, wheeling stacks of $100 bills back and forth in a wooden Civil-War-like cart, "paper handler" it was called, subsistence wages with no retirement, his two other children, a girl of 40 and a boy of 31, were unmarried and nuts. His face turned dark.

"Can't you be in trouble, Grandpa?" said the child.

"O trouble? I need to get in the house, and the door is locked. I need food and I have no money and I don't know what to do."

"That's not trouble, Falseface has to be after you," said the child.

"I should go get a job, that's what I should do!" said Grandpa, laughing his odyssey-less laugh, the Depression would haunt him forever.

"I'll be Cat Woman, you be Falseface," said the child. Grandpa's hearing was not of the best, he was not that conversant with Batman either, and his mind drifted. "I need some money and I can't get in my house," his dental plate cheap and ill-fitting.

"Serena, you'll miss your bus, are you done with your soup, or not?" said the mother.

"Listen to momma," said Grandpa Max.

Kachka wiped the child's mouth with a wash cloth and brushed her hair while the child still ate, then she turned to Grandpa Max and told him she was taking the child to the bus. "I might go somewhere else after I drop

Serena at her bus stop," she said, "If I miss Lou, tell him I'll see him when he gets back from Reno."

Just then, the son returned from his summer teaching job.

"Poppa, I'm teaching Civics. Do you know what I'm teaching? I'm teaching Civics to high school seniors. There's sixteen kids in the class who have to pass this course or else they don't graduate. It's up to me Poppa whether they graduate or not. You wanna hear some questions from this test? Here's some questions, question number one, are you ready?"

"Ready, ready," said the father.

"Karl Marx and the Marxist-Leninists say that wage slavery has to be abolished and they must make the workers see that wage slavery is detrimental to their true self-interest. What do you think?"

Grandpa Max sat in his chair with his legs crossed, smoking his richly flavored aromatic pipe, his only luxury, deep in thought. His fly was open. "Do you have a book that tells you're supposed to teach such things, I know in New York they give teachers a book so they should know what to teach from."

The son laughed. At fifteen, he had been a leader in a Communist front organization for youth. "I'm covered

Poppa, these kids see me and they think I'm the Establishment."

"Sure, sure, I know, but ..."

"Don't worry Poppa, if I'm the one standing up there teaching the course, I must be from the Board of Education, right?"

"Absolutely!" said the father.

The son laughed. The Jewish wife in the kitchen cried. The father sucked on his pipe.

"Look, all these kids are working class kids. They all wanna graduate. I taught them the essence of Jeffersonian democracy. The right answer, do you know the right answer, Poppa?? All these kids are throwing back the right answer, except one, a Chinese girl, and even she chickened out, the right answer. "How do we know who shall lead and who shall be led? Who is to know? Who is so smart to figure it all out? The people! Who can be wiser than the people themselves?"

"Nu shure!" the father said.

The wife ate another summer fruit in the kitchen where nobody could see her. The husband laughed, and the wife knew he was making no breakthru with his sexual problems, as she was making no breakthru with hers.

"Sure! You have to be some jackass to say anything

else, you have to be some jerk! If I was going for a civil service job, I would . . . " said the father. "The funny thing is," said his son, "if a kid gave another answer, I'd probably give him an A, and you know what I'd say?"

Grandpa didn't know.

"I'd write in the margin, "I don't agree with your conclusion, but you have a right to it, and you're thinking, so here's an A."

Two mornings later, after they came back from Reno, Grandpa Max was doing an awful lot of hangin' around, Kachka was going crazy with the old man's pajamas and the fly coming open like that. "Would you like to come with me to buy some fruit now?" she said. She had to use the most formal of tones with him, or else she would explode. His face appeared very dry with sixty-five years of having the wrong thoughts about everything.

"Sure!" he said, "but first I have to go get out of my pajamas."

Pajamas. Pajamas. It was all a question of getting out of your pajamas, she wanted to go away, from all of them, from the father and his son as well, but she sat in their pitiful backyard with her two little girls watching them play with their playdough. She had made a fresh batch for them the day before, had wrapped it in plastic like they did in the nursery school, the safe, safe nursery school, where there was no talk of procuring for your father, your pitiful, toothless old father, with his fly hanging open. There, there was just the magic of childhood and recipes for playdough, flour, salt, a few drops of food coloring, and just enough water to make it all stick together just right.

"I need it, it's mine," said the younger child.

"But I need to play too," said the mother, grabbing a piece of playdough and making a ball out of it.

"Sure, momma's only a little girl too, she needs some little girl toys to play with, momma's only a little girl like you," said Grandpa Max.

When lunch was over, and the cream of asparagus soup had been eaten, and the pieces of cantaloupe eaten as well, Kachka took her children by the hand, said goodbye to Grandpa Max and his son, her husband, and walked with them to the corner of Spruce and Los Angeles to wait for the schoolbus, the big yellow University of California Child Study Center bus. Her little girl got on, wobbled in the aisle for a minute, and then sat down in one of the front window seats. She had dark plenteous hair and perfect baby teeth, and the mother could see her tender little shoulders and arms sticking out of the white cotton dress, sleeveless, with a million strawberries all over it. The child had the joy of life in her, and the mother stared deeply at her child as the bus pulled away.

Then she grabbed the little one's hand, and they both crossed the street to her car and they both got into it, the pale blue Studebaker that was still hanging on for dear life. That being done, the mother snapped the child into her seatbelt, and they both drove around, to nowhere in particular. Maybe she'd scooty-doo on over to Albany High School and sign up for a class in Adult Swim now that it was summer.

* * *

two women

"You really have to do something about your life, . . . my God, you know you can't keep going on like this."

"Yes, I know," I said.

It was a rainy day, and she was 38 and I was 39.

"I mean, you can't really go on the way you have . . . this is no life for you. You're too rich inside, Shayna, you're too warm and gifted a person to have such a dead life, it's such a bloody shame."

I sat there, cross-legged on the floor. I was nodding, wearing my red corduroy pants and my filthy sneakers, (this is a way for a Jewish girl to go out in the street???)

"Like my black friend Bob Jackson used to say, "You gotta get out there lookin' good, you gotta *catch a* little."

"Yes," I said.

"My God, it's such a waste Shayna, it wouldn't even be any trouble for you to do it, you're just naturally so alive, your mind and your soul are so honed, as they say, everyone would just dig you to pieces."

"I know, I think I know what you mean."

"Promise me you'll do something, " said Georgette. "Promise."

"I'm only buggin' you this way because I love you, dear sweet friend, dear sweet person you, it's only because you're so beautiful and so fine and so rich inside that I want to give everyone in the world a chance to love you too, and they would, if they only knew."

"I know," I said.

"You're just too fine to lock yourself up away from the world this way, I want you to get all the love and admiration you deserve."

The day was cold and rainy. It was September. We were sitting in her child's room. The child, a girl of 13, had gone away to England, to go to school there for a year, and Georgette, the mother, was sick over it, or sick with something, sick with not knowing what to do with the rest of her life. For the child's part, she was happy to go somewhere, she was going to be with friends. But for the mother, to be parted like that from her only child, it was dreadful. The mother lay in the child's bed in the child's room. Smoking a cigarette and drinking in the child's sleeping bag.

"You're my best friend," I said, "You're my best friend

and I have nowhere else to go so I came here. I thought because you are my best friend and it is cold and raining out that I would come here and sit down here on your floor and watch you smoke cigarettes in your child's sleeping bag. Actually, I am worried about you. I was driving by and I thought . . . "shit, Georgette's depressed, maybe she's up there killing herself, and I can stop it."

"Did you really think that, dear sweet person?"

"Yes," I said.

"God bless," she said.

I was sitting on the floor and I had my legs crossed and I had my sneakers on and the red corduroy pants. The sneakers were bought the summer before when I decided at the age of thirty-eight and a half that I needed some exercise, and the red pants were from the summer my mother died, right after my mother died, I waltzed over to J.C. Pennys, pronto, and got myself a pair of red corduroy pants. With the sneakers, I had taken six cheap group tennis lessons from the Berkeley Deptartment of Parks and Recreation, and then I had quit, and there was nothing to join and then quit after my mother died, so I bought the red corduroy pants.

"I feel like I'm dyin'," she said. "Like Keats, I'm half in love with easeful death. If we could only just die, if we could only lay down and forget it all."

"Yeah," I said.

I thought of the small piece of thick green phlegm pasted on my mother's oxygen mask in the hospital, with my mother's face all puffy and struggling under the mask. The mask was tiny and lightweight, it looked like a fancy pair of Italian sunglasses that you could buy in the Notions Department of Bloomingdales, except it came over your nose and your mouth instead of over your eyes, and it was a prison, it might just as well have been steel bars separating my mother from me and from the rest of the world.

I'm sitting on the floor in someone's bedroom, I said to myself, is that all there is?

"What should I do?" I said.

"You have to have a few good times," she said. "You have to go out and find yourself a few good times."

"OK," said Shayna, who was me, while all the pussycats and horses, all the fur-robed kings and bearded witches, all the fine books of poetry liberal people give to little girls, and all the photographs on walls, all those fine photographs of fine people at picnics, children and grownups, smiling from beaches, stuffing sandwiches into their mouths, couldn't agree with me more.

"I hear you," I said.

"I don't mean to be hard on you babe, I don't mean to be coming down hard on you like some old aunt with hairs coming out of her chin (always something deprecating about women!) I just want you to be happy, that's all. Don't you agree with me that you must do something about this mess you're in, or are you . . . satisfied to . . ."

"I don't know," I said.

"Come on Shayna, come on, you're my best friend, can you really be satisfied with so little? If you weren't so rich inside, if you didn't have such a finely honed intellect, I mean, don't look at me, I'm just an old clumsy whore who drinks too much, you don't have to take anything I say seriously."

"Please, Georgette, please, you're not a whore."

"Well, we're all whores, darling. In one way or another. I haven't said anything so terrible, have I?"

"You have to go out and get yourself a beau," she said at last, "at least that. I'm not saying that's the answer to everything, to art and poetry and the ultimate loneliness of your Jewish soul or anything, O come on, I don't just mean getting laid, I mean someone to love you, someone to appreciate you and hold your hand on a walk through the woods, someone to tell you how funny you are because you thought up a terribly funny word, or just someone who'll gently wind your sideburns, or whatever you call them, behind your ears, when your hair is falling in your eyes."

"Yeah, sideburns."

"I mean you just can't get that from women, Shayna, you just can't get it from women."

"OK" I said.

"I mean a woman can't hold you the way a man can, a woman can't fuck you at night."

"Sure!" ('vu den'?)

"I'm telling you the truth, Shayna, you can have all these fine conversations with women, you can be so attuned till it's comin' out of your fanny, darling, and then..."

"Yeah, and then?"

"And then you need something else," said Georgette.

"Like a good stiff prick," I said.

"No, not a good stiff prick, the prick is the least of it, silly, I mean just someone who appreciates your mind, who you can sleep with at night."

"O," I said.

"Shayna, listen to me, listen," she pleaded. "Don't take any example from me, everyday since my child's been gone, since my child left me, Jesus only knows, Jesus forgive me, I've boozed myself into oblivion, I've crept out of this fucking house like a snake creeping through the bayou at night, creeping around to the Albatross totally smashed, creeping back home with some decent black man with a gold tooth in the front of his mouth, no, I mean it, who can't even speak the English language, to say nothing of understanding my feelings, the poor fool. But I needed to have something from a man, some affection, another body on mine."

"Oh God," I sighed, thinking of her nights. "Is there anything to eat in this house?"

". . . and it's awful, it's devastating, I tell you no lie, waking up in the morning with that man, with the gold tooth in his mouth. Why, there's nothing to say, dear friend, nothing. And I'm so ugly and fat and miserable and hungover and lined, it's all I can do to pretend I'm half-asleep and put my hair over my eyes like this so the poor fool won't get to see my face, it's awful, Shayna."

She put her hair over her face like all the Japanese actresses in Rashomon.

"So the poor sap can't see how old I am, how bad I look."

Her hair hung over her face and you couldn't see her eyes at all, and she said in a cracked, sexy, morning voice.

"Can I get you some coffee, Rudy? I think there's a

little cold cereal in the closet, would you like some of that? I don't know what you usually eat for breakfast . . ."

"Shayna, I don't know what to say to get rid of them in the morning."

"I think there's a little dried cereal in the house, would you like me to get you some of that?"

I sat there laughing at her performance. She had it down so well. She had performed this performance for me many times, and she knew it was good, and she knew I liked it, and she knew, she knew everything.

"Can I get you some coffee?" She was barely audible now in her sexy whisper, and with her hair over her eyes, hiding her face. "Can I get you some coffee, do you take anything with it? Or do you have yours black?"

". . . there's a little cereal in the pantry closet . . ."

"Believe me, I don't bring home prizes anymore . . . but the booze, the booze just gets me out there, believe me, dear friend, I have to be absolutely smashed before I can fuck anyone."

What was there to say?

"Darling, I love you," she said. "You're my dearest, dearest friend, there are three women I love in this world, my mother, who is a fine old lady of 81, an idealist who works tirelessly for her ideals, League of Women Voters, the Margaret Sanger Clinic, and such; my child, who is a true innocent living abroad in England, probably wearing a middy blouse playing rugby in a field somewhere right now; and you, dear sweet you, Shayna, you, right here in this house with me right now. You do agree with me, you do agree," she was saying, "that you must after all do something about your life NOW, or you must forever be content with this silence and death, death and silence, well then, who am I . . ."

She took a drink from her glass.

"Who am I but a miserable, garrulous, 38 year old whore who is overweight to the bargain."

"You're not a whore," I said.

"All right, I won't say it if you don't want me to, but I know who I am. I called up some guy before you came and made an appointment for Friday, Stanley Wiseman, Dr. Stanley Wiseman, the Bio-Energetics man, he's gonna see me on Friday, I'm really scared now, Shayna, I'm really scared."

"That sounds OK," I said. ('it shouldn't hoit')

"I'm really scared."

She started to cry.

"I'm glad you called," I said.

"I had to," she said. "I didn't know what else to do,

Oh, you don't know, you just don't know, I wake up every night and start trembling so. Snakes and scary things from Ray Milland's *Lost Weekend* start crawling out of the walls, and there's nothing I can do, I mean nothing, to get myself back to sleep again."

"It's a good idea, I'm glad you called," I said.

"You know," she puffed on her cigarette and drank her booze, "these little Bio-Energetics men, they're like a little group of elves who've come to repair us in the middle of the night, marching, marching. With satchels full of hammers and other little tools . . . they don't talk to you anymore."

Her nose was running, and her snot was running into her orange juice and vodka. (gey, nemzich a hanky!)

"You just go there and say a few words to them, and then you do some exercise and go home."

"Perfect," I said feeling very Jewish, "that can't hurt."

"You'd know his name would have to be WISE MAN," she said. She blew her nose, coughed, and took another drink of her vodka.

"Instead of doing my number for these sad and lonely black men, I'll do it for Dr. Wise Ass, I mean, Dr. Wise Man. Only him I'll have to pay to catch my act."

"You pay the others too," I said.

She started to cry again.

"We all pay for our performance," I said.

"Please Georgette, please, I love you, we'll marry in an avant-garde ballet, every night I'll make two ponytails in your hair and put a blue satin ribbon in each one, we'll walk through rainforests together, in a commercial, please, Georgette please, let me bring you warm Ovaltine in a Yahrzeit glass and brush your hair 100 strokes, and read you *Dick Tracy* and *Nancy Drew, The Mystery of the Secret Clock,* please, Georgette, please, eat your matzoball soup it's getting cold eat, while you lounge in your little girl's sleeping bag, eat! eat!

She was starting to go into her incredible performance again, she had the whole black tone and voice down so fine.

"You know what they tell me after I commit carnal relations with them, which means after I fuck them and go down on them and get absolutely nothing in return?" (gottenyu, a coorva!)

"Georgette!" I cried.

"It's all right, I don't care, I can get by without coming. God, you'd think they'd know how to take care of business, for all their jiving."

"Georgette, Georgette . . . I love you!"

"They say to me... 'Georgette! Mama! Where you been, you so real, Georgette, you some real people, how come I never met you before?"

She cried and laughed and farted into the child's sleeping bag.

"Maybe you can go to an encounter group too," she said. "Maybe you can go to the one I'm going to, you can come to Dr. Wise Ass with me, and we can do Bio-energetics together,"

"No," I said, "it's better if you go alone."

"How did you know? I've been dyin' to get into a group where nobody knows me, where nobody has ever seen me before"

"I know," I said, omniscient. "Would you like me to close the windows? It's really cold in here." The windows were wide open and the rain was coming in.

"Yes, please," she said, blowing her nose, "would you? I just have to stop popping these pills and drinking. Do you know how many pills I've taken this week?"

"No," I said.

"I'm killing myself, I'm just killing myself."

"Promise me, Georgette, promise me you won't take the pills anymore."

"I have no energy I have no energy!" she cried. "I take

them because I can't do a thing when I wake up in the morning. I can't touch the place, look at it, I haven't been able to lift a dish in three weeks, I lost $31 calling in sick today."

"But they don't do you any good, Georgette, promise me that at least you won't drink and pop the pills together, that's all I ask. Drink if you have to, or take the pills, just don't do both at the same time."

"I've thrown down about 100 of them just this week,"

"Promise me."

"I'm scared now, I'm really scared this time," she said, "you don't know how long this has been going on."

I got up and closed all the windows and I went to the kitchen to look for food. "Is there anything to eat in this house?" I called into the other room.

"There's not a scrap of food in the house," she called back from the bed. "I haven't done a bit of shopping in three weeks, I just don't eat food anymore. I think there's some orange juice in the freezer if you want it."

"That's okay," I said, "I'm not hungry anyway."

"Well, at least you don't drink," she called through the rooms.

I came back into the bedroom and sank back down to the floor again, resuming my cross-legged position.

"What do you really want to do?" she asked. "Isn't there something you really want to do?"

"Oh, I don't know," I said, quite musically.

"If you could only have some fun."

"So what's fun?" I asked.

"Well, you know, like Carlene Berkowitz, this past weekend, she went down to the Monterey Jazz Festival... she spent a weekend there with her new lover, Axelrod, and she had a marvelous time with him. And then, she's always making booking engagements for her friend, Reno." Reno was a jazz musician Carlene was always making booking engagements for.

"She's always going places, always doing things, a trip to Boston when she's tired of teaching, a month in Mexico, always having people over for dinner, always places to go, things to do, always a dialogue with other people, and moving, moving in the real world. With people close by."

"I'm not Carlene Berkowitz." ('Carlene, this is a name for a Jewish girl?')

"I didn't say you were."

"I don't dig her kind of fun. She's very male-oriented, for one thing," I tried to sound like I had some political conviction, or any other kind of conviction.

"She has some high school prom idea of fun, that's

not me."

"That's not you? What in the world are you talking about, Shayna?"

"Look, she sells her birthright for a pinch on her ass, or a roll in the hay, that's not me, that's not who I am."

"Then who the fuck are you, you poor dumb ass?"

"I'm a Jew, you shmuck, I'm a Jew. I hate the system, do you know? You don't know who I am, do you? I hate the system, hahahaha, you don't know me, it's funny, I hate the system, but you don't know."

"What system? What system?" she winced, becoming Jewish right before my eyes.

"The system! The system! Males buying females! Auction blocks! Dominance gestures! Gestures of submission! I will not serve. Non serviam, Georgette, non serviam. I will not serve, get it? I will have no "idols before thee," get it? No idols Georgette, get it? Get it Georgette, I will not kiss ass."

"But you have to have some fun!" she cried. "There has to be something you're looking forward to!"

"I'm looking forward to me."

"Then stay home and tickle your own Yiddische clitoris," she cried, "see if I care!" (oy, my Jewish cunt is showing!)

"I don't see it that way, Georgette, I just don't see it that way. You know, it's like a scene out of Thomas Mann. He always has these desolate German middle-aged men on desolate afternoons in a deserted park. The old guy sits down on a bench and he knows his life has been a waste, and he hears some kids playing, the kids play their games right under his nose, without even seeing him, he's such a non-entity, and he is DEPRESSED, as only a solid middle-class German burgher can be depressed, true angst, European, and he feels the waste of it, and he really feels it, and he sobs into his big old German winter coat, and he leaves the park just as the sun is setting and the cold is coming in, he's going home maybe to some loyal spinster sister who's cooked him a hot German supper, and he leaves the park, REBORN! Well, I dig the nothingness, but I'm only 39 and a half, I'm not 55 yet, can you dig it? I'm only in the middle of the long dark night of the soul, and I dig the nothingness! I dig it to pieces. But there is no redemption for me. I DO NOT LEAVE THE PARK 'REBORN' I'm not ready to be reborn, I guess."

"Stop it, stop this talk I don't want to hear any more!"

"I know," I said.

"There has to be something you wanna do, there has to be something you're looking forward to, you can't go on like this! You can't take on the system by yourself!"

"It's all right," I smiled sheepishly, like a know it-all.

"There hasta be something you wanna do, even if it's just going to the library to get out a book on macramé. Shayna! You have to do something, you just can't let yourself die!"

"I won't die," I lied. "So what's so bad about dying? We all die someday, in some place, in some way or other. I saw my mother die this summer and it didn't stop me. What do you mean by that just die? Everybody just dies, that's the way you die, you just die."

She started to cry and sob into the sleeping bag and I felt what an ass I am just farting up her afternoon.

I'm sorry, Georgette, I'm sorry, I'm just feeling a little low today, I shouldn't have come by to lay it all on you. I'll go home now."

"You don't have to go home," she said.

"I'm poisoning your afternoon," I said.

"You're not poisoning my afternoon, my afternoon was already poisoned long before you got here."

"I don't know," I said. "I'm too high to need a good time, and I'm too depressed to know I'm missing one."

"Just don't talk about how happy you are with your precious Jewish sadness, please, just don't talk about it.

"All right, I won't talk about it."

"How about a walk?" I said.

"Yeah, yeah, a walk might be fine. But won't you be too cold? You're feeling cold as it is."

"No, I'll be fine," I said. "I think I'll make a wee wee in the john first."

I got up off the floor.

"I think I'll make a wee wee too," she said, drying her eyes.

I waited for her in the foyer while she went to the bathroom. An ashtray full of butts fell over on the floor when my arm accidentally knocked it over. All the butts and ashes were lying there on the beige carpeting when she came out of the john zipping up her fly.

"My god! I weigh a ton," she said. "I must do something about my weight."

She saw me on my hands and knees, picking up ashes.

"Oh, you knocked the ashtray over," she said.

"I'm getting it all, don't worry."

"Wasn't there a lighted cigarette there too?"

She threw her London Fog over the blue jeans and sweater. "Be sure you get the lighted one," she chirped. "I may hate this place, but I'm not ready to burn it down yet."

"Don't worry, I'm getting it all."

I rubbed the beige carpet till there was only the shadow of a stain.

"Are we about ready?" she chirped again.

I hunched myself up, I could hardly stand.

"Wow, I could sure use some of that Bio-Energetics. You look beautiful, Georgette, classical, the Vassar girl, Twenty Years Later." ('a shiksa! a shiksa! she is after all, a shiksa!')

"Vassar girl, shit! I put my head in the oven so they'd send me home from Vassar"

We walked the soggy streets, the rainy light was dazzling. A reliable collie dog, well bred and courteous, walked past us, stopping first to let us pass.

"Isn't it fine?" she said.

"Yes, isn't it a fine day to visit Madeline?"

That got a laugh out of her.

"I always liked the rain, these are my favorite days," she said. "I could never live in an apartment house again."

"Do you want to go home now?" I said. We hadn't walked more than two blocks.

"Yes," she said, "yea, I really must get home."

This time, as we turned, another serious dog walked towards us, not nearly as courteous as the first. In the rainy distance, children at the corner, a child in a yellow raincoat and red rubber boots, maybe four years old.

"I'm glad you called the Bio-Energetics man," I said.

"I'm not in it yet, he has to look me over to see if I fit into his group. If he doesn't think I fit, I can't get in. It's sixty dollars, Shayna, sixty dollars a month, I don't see how I'll do it, I have no bread."

"Just go," I said, "please."

By the time we got to the corner, my mouth had grown dry as a desert. The child jumped out at us, trying to scare us and show off for her friends. They all opened their mouths to show us they had swallowed rain.

"I'll never dress a kid of mine up in an outfit like that again, no kid of mine will ever be that age again," I said.

"What about me? I only have one, at least you have three," she said. "They're still small, they need you, at least you have a reason for living,"

I couldn't find my car when we got back to her house.

"Where'd you park it?" she asked.

"Right here. I parked it right in front of your house."

It was a white car, like so many other white cars that year in California, but the back of it was all scarred and studded with a huge plaster mess that I had just never gotten around to covering up.

"There it is, I see it!" I said.

She stood for a moment and watched me get into my car. And I stood there too, watching her watch me.

"I really must go upstairs and get myself back into bed," she said.

"I know," I said, "thanks."

And since I didn't know what to thank her for, I cried out, "Thanks! Thanks for helping me find my car!"

I started it up and headed home.

* * *

death to the fascist imperialist dogs

She got up earlier than usual, and got herself ready to go to the all-women's Breakaway Massage Workshop. She had heard of women waking in the dead of night, bracing themselves for the day ahead with very strong French Roast coffee, sitting quietly in their kitchens, alone in half-darkness, thinking their thoughts, plotting their Breakaway. She sat alone in her dark kitchen, it was a Saturday morning, making Rose Hips tea, wondering whether to go or not, not that it was such a big deal either way. Her life didn't change somehow whether she went to things or stayed home, opening the door didn't really do it for her.

She strained the Rose Hips with a strainer and sat drinking it very hot, at least it was a strong sensation. The children were in the TV room, and there was no fighting or anything, they weren't bothering her or calling to her, or asking her for things, but she had to hurry, she had to make a quick breakaway if she wanted anything for herself, at any moment, she'd be crushed. She felt she was some kind of wind-up toy, really, a tiny toy a child's small hand might hold, there she was, and there was the little world, and anyone could wind it up, and she'd be condemned to a sea of wild spastic movements. Unless she got the jump on the machine. She strained off another cup of tea.

It was a Saturday, the children were all watching The Jackson Five, already idolizing the male rock stars of eight and ten and eleven years old. "Look," said her five year old, "he's doing the pussy, he wants to stick it in." Her three little girls sat on the couch in their flannel nightgowns and their quilted nylon acetate robes, transfixed, eating their Fruit Loops, their little mouths slack, their dark eyes feverish as they sat and watched, and once or twice, they ran back to the kitchen with their empty, nonbreakable bowls, their nylon housecoats flying, like little queens rushing down draughty corridors.

She had a splitting headache. Ever since she had turned forty really, she had had the most perpetual flu. "Do you have any flu symptoms?" asked the nurse at the desk at Kaiser Hospital, when she was driven finally to go get a checkup.

She dialed her friend Gina on the phone.

"Gina, this is Gloria, did I wake you?"

"Oh hi, good morning," said Gina, she had managed somehow to stifle her entire existential reality.

"What are you doing right now?"

Gloria had a habit of calling her woman friends (she had none other) and asking them what they were doing right now. Then, listening good and hard, she created an eternity for their answer to resound in. This was just one special trick she had. Gina said that two kids were away at the Boy Scouts and two were home, and she was sitting it out till evening when Nora was invited to another kid's house, and Alex would have a babysitter. And then, at that time, she, Gina, was going off to Inverness to see a friend.

So much for divorced mothers.

"Oh, so you're going to see a friend?"

"I like going to see friends, I'll stay the night."

Gina saw a psychiatrist twice a month. She had been instructed to save up her problems on little pieces of paper so she could remember them.

"Yes, I like change. I like to do things. I've paid dearly to push myself out the door and visit a friend. It's something I recommend. I heartily recommend pushing yourself out the door and visiting a friend, if you can spend the night away from home, so much the better. My psychiatrist turned me on to it, your basic low-cost getaway."

Yes, that's what psychiatrists and their ilk always advised, go out the door, enjoy the sun, enjoy a walk, why not get a bike? Go to a movie, even if you're lonely, haven't you heard, there are characters to identify with? Or, "why are you so down on yourself?" that was another old standby. Through her psychiatrist, Gina had been forewarned of certain existential realities, that all she had to do was get rid of the kids, step into her little red sports car (all divorced women have little red sports cars, haven't you noticed? laughed Gina) and go off somewhere, like any well-dressed upper-class French woman in the movies.

"I have a chance to go to this massage weekend," said Gloria.

"How fantastic! Go!" said Gina.

"It's something given through Breakaway, you've heard of that new school that opened up for women?"

"Oh yes, yes."

"But I have this splitting headache. I don't know whether to go or not. I think I have the flu."

"Just go," said Gina.

"I don't know. I go to these things and then I can't

wait till they're over so I can come home."

"Well at least that's a reason to come home."

"Really?"

"Of course. Besides, what will you do otherwise?"

"The kids are bored and fighting. Is it like that Saturday mornings at your house?"

"Oh yes, but you know me, the trick is getting out the door, why don't you go and then you can call me up afterwards and we can talk about it?"

"It's all right . . . I was just reaching out . . ."

"Don't worry about it. Call me up later, I'd love to hear."

Gloria got the large Fieldcrest pink bath towel and went upstairs to tell Steven about Julie's medicine.

"I wrote up a schedule," she said, "I wrote it all out, it's on the kitchen table. She gets the Marax and the Atarax at noon and at four, and give her the mycin, that's the one in the frigidaire, give her that one at two. Be sure you shake up the one in the frigidaire. And use a measuring spoon so she gets the full dosage." She held up the measuring spoons and jiggled them at him while he lay in bed. "Look, this is the teaspoon, use this one, don't give her this, this is the tablespoon."

"OK, fine, fine, remember to be back by seven."

"OK," she said.

She hated him because he had a standing date with a medical secretary every Saturday night. Every Saturday, he would put on his black leather vest with the gold buttons, take a shower, splash lots of after-shave lotion on himself and be off, off to see his medical secretary, probably someone over in the city, while, she, Gloria, the wife, came home from where she had been, which was nowhere, and scream, "You lousy fuckers, get to bed already!" at the children, "get the fuck to bed before I beat you." In her mind, she would have her plans for a quiet evening, some special quiet in which she could finally "get her head together." Maybe she would read, maybe she would write, maybe she'd get stoned and watch a late movie, and catch, from some carelessly dropped little phrase from the lips of Humphrey Bogart, the key to her destiny. She nurtured a desire to divorce her husband, once and for all, a desire for what was called heavy changes, she wanted to kick him out and start to live, but she believed none of it, none of that live your own life talk. And, of course, she was afraid. She had seen her share of enough divorced women of forty.

But of course, she did none of these quiet evening things, for every time after he splashed himself with his cologne, and she watched him, she watched him out of the corners of her million eyes, after he had said, "I'll be back late Sunday evening". . . and after she had said, "Fine, have a wonderful time, I don't care if I don't see you till next June," after all these marvelous words, uttered to show that she was, after all, her own person, he slammed the big front door, and she threw herself across the bed and cried.

After a third cup of Rose Hips tea, Gloria kissed each child goodbye, reminding them all each one to "bus your own dish and give Mommy a kiss," and left the house. Ah, it was so nice out, so nice outside, so different than the weather inside. Her youngest child had bronchitis and asthma and she had to give her the antibiotic three times a day, and then there was the anti-wheeze medicine, four times a day, and the child was restless and didn't want to stay in the house anymore. Ah, for freedom. Forty she was, and she didn't feel that good, but she could still feel something, something free now and then. On and on she walked, on and on, the walk was really just five or six blocks long, but she had a way of making herself think she was alone in a jungle passing by lions and tigers, protecting her thoughts from their drooling fangs. It didn't look too good in Mary's Coffeeshop, so she didn't stay. But wait, there's Merv Figaro, he has a job teaching at SF State now, there he is saying hello, isn't that a strange mustard color pants he's wearing, baggy mustard color pants, and he's got a green velvet belt to go with it, why is he wearing a belt with his pants down so low, that's weird, and where did he ever find that mustard color anyway? God, those pants are baggy! There he goes with a queer-looking guy, I bet he's out of the closet now. Well, good for him, he sure stayed in that closet long enough, look, they're both out on a Saturday morning, each carrying a small bag of laundry to the laundromat. Nothing like her bags of laundry. How touching. No one bothered to look up when she walked into *Mary's*, she had stopped getting looks a while back. She was too old, too dowdy, she could not compete with the young girls looking swell in jeans and skinny rib knit turtleneck sweaters. Usually these children wore crazy Italian shoes with high heels under their jeans, purple suede platforms or sleek brown leather, something from a machismo fantasy. Yes, they were children, she thought, all the young girls are little girls, and all the men are really little boys. Once, she had gone to a Monday night divorced encounter group, (though not yet divorced herself), and a rugged-looking man was telling everyone how he had survived alone in the woods for 10 days. "Wasn't that one cute?" her friend Jolie had said when they left, but

Gloria could only see him as an aggressive four-year-old boy-child in a nursery school, fighting over the wheel toys.

No, no one held their breath over her, too dowdy to get a look, she didn't stay long at *Mary's*, but ambled on to the drugstore next door to get her cake of cocoa butter. "Bring a towel, a foam rubber pad to lay on, and some cocoa butter," said Ferne, the massage leader. Ferne was political, she had a heightened political consciousness. She was giving the massage workshop free because that's what you did when you had a heightened political consciousness. At the drugstore counter was the local poet who had reached a modest fame, hardly the big time . . . still pushing at fifty. He taught English at the University, all the snooty courses you had to prove yourself in, before they let you in. He looked like he had lost a lot of weight lately, like he was on a vegetarian diet, had changed over from being a heavy meat and potatoes eater to a grains and vegetables man, why would his pants be hanging on him like this otherwise? This is a day for seeing strangers with baggy pants, said Gloria, the second one I saw today, with baggy pants, going about his business. The girl at the drug counter, dressed in white like a nurse, was punching the cash register for the macrobiotic poet who held $4.35 worth of cartridge ball point refills in his hands. He looked glum.

The day was gorgeous It was a great day to be out fucking and whoring and blowing the mind of some young idolatrous girl who wants to write poetry, his being vibrated, there are many such who would adore me, make me a soufflé or a fondue, cook me a curried eggplant, wash a sock or two.

"$4.35," said the girl, "would you like a bag?"

"No thanks, I'll just carry them."

He stuffed all the cartridges into his two front pants pockets, said thank you with a studied high-level cosmic consciousness, the way any decent self-respecting evolved type would, aware of all our cycles of birth and rebirth, and, like a good Buddha, left the drugstore without a fuss.

But Gloria, in this small town, knew another side of him, before the advance of his vegetarian middle age, which wasn't fooling anyone. Her friend Grace had had this same baggy-panted poet for a lover when she was a mere 19, and he was 39. He had come tearing into her furnished room, leaving his wife at home with the usual excuse about work to do in his Dwinelle Hall Office. Grace had been a mere child with pubic hair like gentle rain from heaven, falling, thrice blessed, upon the place beneath. He would lunge into her room in the student quarter and throw a small bag of shoulder lamb chops and frozen peas on the table top. It was all timed so he could throw four lamb chops in the broiler, fuck her, get up and throw the peas in the water, come back to bed for a second try, and, by that time, the peas would be done. They would sit and eat together, and then he would go home. What a small town this was, she thought, you stand next to somebody buying cartridge refills in a drugstore and you know all about his shoulder lamb chops and his frozen peas.

On she trudged to the massage, would her headache ever go away? The workshop was being held at the other end of town, and she welcomed the walk there. It was supposed to be at the home of a Quaker attendant, a woman who was volunteering the free use of her livingroom floor for the massage workshop. Gloria mused over this as she carried her towel and cake of Hershey's cocoa butter, and if she had had a better place to go, she would have gone there.

She stopped at the little Japanese grocery at the corner of Rose and Grove and bought herself a ten cent bag of salted pumpkin seeds in the shell, and walked along, sucking salt and littering.

Why didn't she want to go to these things? She just didn't. It seemed really when you looked at it, she had no place to go, there was no PLACE for her, really. She could not stay home, she was tormented there, and everywhere she went seemed so antiseptic to her. She would sign up for all sorts of Free University classes, people would ask her what she was taking at the Free U, and she would say "sculpture and ceramics, the tarot deck and how to fix your VW bus yourself, carpentry, the caballah, Bob Dylan's lyrics, and female sexuality," to say nothing of yoga therapy, chanting OM, Gestalt encounter, creative writing and Theater Games. But she could never stay with any of these things. In the class, she would always find herself struggling to listen, struggling to see the demonstration of a technique, just a little slow, just a little out of it, a nearsighted face in the background, straining to understand. She would always drop out behind her glasses and her unplucked eyebrows, rolling the little ball which was her life in her hands, warming it up so it could be ready to take shape at a moment's notice, so to speak.

Maureen had called her yesterday, why had she called? She was so mad at Maureen. She had called with a terrible story. "Gloria, Gloria," she had whispered hoarsely on the phone, "I have something to tell you, something awful has happened to me, are you busy? Can you talk now?"

"Sure, sure," said Gloria, "what happened?"

Gloria was always ready to listen to Maureen tell her stories. Maureen knew how to lay a good story on you, and she was always having "adventures". In the space of the two years she had lived in this small town, Maureen had covered all the night scenes and the day scenes, especially in the world of sex and lovers was Maureen not at all a journeyman or an apprentice. Whereas Gloria would stay home, all I do, she would say at the start of one of her haiku poems, is stay home . . . she would say "stay home" like people who do meditation say "sitting." She would throw these pieces of paper she wrote on in a drawer where she kept old red nylon garter belts she never wore anymore, but somehow didn't have the heart to throw away. Yes, Gloria stayed home. And Maureen went out. While Maureen was out picking up lovers, Gloria could be found browsing through the book section of Wholly Foods, or Infinity Foods, or the Woman's Bookstore, and she would come home with a small recycled brown paper bag of short grain Chico brown rice, Mu Tea, and a pamphlet called *Do-In, the Art of Self-Massage,* or maybe a copy of *Diet For a Small Planet,* or the *Writings of Huang Po (the Zen Philosophy of Non-Attainment),* for what, after all, did she have to attain? Or *Zen Cookery.* For all this, Maureen was out getting lovers, yes, yes, always lovers, that Maureen, she was no fool, she knew that life was lovers, not organic gardening or body alignment. Not drop-in Friday night Psychodrama, or Ecology Action. That Maureen, she knew, life was lovers, it was not going to an all woman's massage, it was not standing in your kitchen mixing up complementary portions of wheat noodles and soy grits. Gloria would learn two recipes in the time it took Maureen to go through two or three lovers. The two had stopped being close friends. Gloria had told her she didn't want to listen anymore, there was something vaguely insulting to Gloria about Maureen's sex stories. She had loved Maureen. One night, they had both been in the livingroom, Steven had gone upstairs to bed and Barbara Shotts was in the next room. Now there was a male-identified woman if ever there was one, that Barbara Shotts! She was nuts, Barbara was, about Mark. She had waited on him like a geisha at a snow inn, she had worked 12 and 14 hours a day as a licensed masseuse and had given Mark all her money, while he, Mark, who had a classification with the Welfare Department known as "socially unemployable" had sat at home playing 12-string guitar, and. . . voila!! He had even bought an airplane with Barbara Shotts' money. Eventually, he married a younger, prettier girl too, but he never gave Barbara Shotts back her airplane.

They had all been sitting in the living room together, Barbara Shotts had just come back from seeing her mother in Ohio, she had run right home when Mark wrote her that he was seeing another woman. Mark had visited Barbara Shotts that very evening, she had given him a blowjob in the room adjoining the living room, Gloria knew because she had come in to close the window, there was a draught coming in . . . and there was Barbara Shotts on her knees giving Mark a blow job, making a slight sucking noise like a baby. Barbara Shotts, she thought she could win him back from the other woman with all sorts of geisha touches, but Mark went and married the other girl anyway. Despite countless blow jobs. Despite Geisha efforts to protect him from stress and interruption. Mark had just gone home to his other girl. Barbara Shotts was in the next room sobbing, Steven had gone to bed, and Gloria and Maureen were sitting in the livingroom having contempt for Barbara. They both got drunk and before Gloria knew it, they were making love to each other. To spite Barbara Shotts. Almost to spite Barbara Shotts, Maureen thrust her hand into Gloria's vagina. Gloria had never felt such a wonderful thing. Maureen went down on Gloria.

"What about Barbara Shotts, she's in the next room."

"What about her?"

"She can hear everything!" whispered Gloria.

"Let her hear!" said Maureen.

So that's what they thought of Barbara Shotts, Barbara Shotts with her little country ways, with her infinite nurturing of the male, she had to be hearing it all in the next room, that's where it's at baby, we're gonna let you have it, where's your little cosmos now, Barbara Shotts?

But that was only one time.

Maureen had come to Gloria the next day and apologized hopelessly. She was drunk, she didn't know what she was doing, it won't happen again, forgive her for being so disgusting, she was so ugly, she said, her ugliness was amazing, was total, shameful, cosmic, bizarre, her ugliness was the ugliness of creeping creatures with piss for blood and livers for eyes. She had a monster's dawning dim awareness of her ugliness, but she hadn't opened herself to the possibility of ugliness everywhere, ugliness as a human possibility, ugliness as a form of awareness. Gloria thought of the personals column she had seen that week in the Women's Newsletter. "Lifeloving feminist and her boychild of four, into organic nibbling, ugly awareness, and high energy, seeks loving home."

"You're so fine, you're so fine and decent, and I'm so

full of filth," argued Maureen.

Gloria and Maureen stayed close friends, their friendship mainly Maureen's revelations of the night before. Gloria always listened, she listened so well, she made Maureen believe in her own life, she was such a good listener. But in her heart, Gloria did not think she had a life, and she was ashamed. Ashamed down to her very soul, down to the depths of her. She figured out how to make squash pie using no sugar or honey, but in her heart, she cringed, ashamed. So the two stopped seeing each other.

"Why do you tell me these things?" asked Gloria, one day on the phone.

"Because I love you, because I have nobody to talk to, because nobody else will listen the way you do. Because I am so worthless. Because I am ashamed."

"I don't like it. I don't dig it anymore. Can't you see? I feel myself drifting from you."

"You feel yourself drifting? You've got your nerve! I come over with chicken and spare ribs, I buy your kids $20 birthday presents, and you feel yourself drifting from me?"

"Yes, I feel myself drawing back."

"Well draw back, fucker, and have a good time doing it. I have been good and kind and decent to you. I have been your friend."

For her part, Gloria never really explained it to herself or to Maureen. She didn't understand it. It was too deep to understand. My shame is too great, wrote Gloria in another Housewife Haiku. My shame is too great/ having no lovers/ come/ should be dripping down my leg/ instead/ soy sauce/ drips down through the crack in the kitchen table/, and in another one, she said "I stand here/ baking squash pies/ there is nothing to attain/", and she threw them all into her drawer with her red silk underpants and garter belts, she must hide these insane confessions of inferiority from the husband she longed to divorce, the children she fed and gave medicines to, whom she wished to run away from.

Her shame was really not so strange. It was a sexual shame. After all, she was violating the First Commandment for Women, fuck and be fucked. She was violating that commandment and she felt guilt. Oh, she knew better.

She knew blah blah blah and blah blah blah, how we were all so socialized and blah blah blah blah, but say what she would, say, "Celibacy is a political act of revolution," say "these good little daddies' girls who believe in mops, mortgages, and baby shit, while SCUM, the Society for Cutting Up Men, small bands of women prowling the face of the earth prowling for emotional thrills," etc. Say what you will, Valerie Solanas was in the nut house, that said it all. Say what you will, talk revolution from sunup to sundown, she would sit in her dentist's office and Cosmopolitan mag would whisper (while the fishes swam in the office aquarium O, those Japanese dentists!) that your body will curl up and become one decaying mass of paranoia if you're not touched, if you're not being fucked by a man. Accommodating women! She could puke! yet they ruled her life.

And poor Maureen, Maureen knew this. She knew that there was no other adventure in life, there is no adventure of the mind, there is no intellectual adventure, there is no adventure of the soul, there is no "keeping straight" adventure, there is one adventure and that is the adventure of come dripping down your leg. It's not the fuck, she would say, it's the talks that go along with it.

And of course, she was right, as Gloria knew in her heart. For each hour she spent reading about acupuncture in Infinity Foods, her friend was having a fuck and a post-coital conversation to match. But each woman in her heart grew more desperate. Gloria gave up her sugarless zen cookery and plunged madly into the meat and sugar scene. She got fat and sick and pre-diabetic, and Maureen drank more and started doing more desperate things. Woman, get thee to a nunnery, said Shakespeare, and he knew.

Gloria arrived at the massage workshop with the pink bath towel and the cake of Hershey's cocoa butter. The women were all young. There were even young girls who lived in the dorms, but even these dorms girls had what was called a feminist consciousness. There were 14 bodies present, that meant seven bodies on the floor being worked, everyone worked in pairs. Everyone loosened up eventually and Gloria lay on the floor getting kneaded and smoothed, small concentric circles growing larger, the bottom hand an ellipse, the top hand a circle, "the ellipse travels, the circle crosses the ellipse," demonstrated the massage leader. She lay on the floor on her pink bath towel, in her head, words... Cosmos, Where is Your Order?

The girl who worked on her was Pat, a divorced woman with two children. She had large pimply nipples, fat that spilled over, stretch marks and green bikini pants, a large girl with a hurt face. Two young lesbians were on the floor, one told how she had just started her radical psychiatry-for-gay-women-group last night. Energy rip off, gay, alternative schools, rip off, rip off, rip off. "He rips off my emotional energy," said a young girl. "I told him to cool it, I told him to fuck off, he was ripping off my energy," said a young girl who looked like a child to Gloria. She found it hard to believe that these children had had such searing emotional experiences. Here and there, she found girls who looked like her oldest daughter, Quintana, ten years old. She was hated, and soothed. Lunch was sent out for.

Everybody chipped in 75 cents and a yogurt and fruit contingent went out to the Westbrae Health Market to bring back food. Gloria lay on the floor too ashamed to say she had no strength to massage anybody, that all she wanted was to be massaged. She lay on the floor, one of 14 bodies in a tiny livingroom, thinking of Maureen, Maureen and her men, always men, she had even started w/young boys, "Can you talk a minute? Can you listen?"

"Why don't you tell your new boyfriend, what's his name, your new 22 year old boyfriend?"

"Oh, Roy, he's a dear, I can't tell him. I don't wanna dump any ugliness on him, besides, he's over in Stinson playing baseball for the weekend, it would really be silly to call or write. Forgive me, dear, for wanting to dump it all on you."

Gloria lay on the tiny living room floor, the large hurt girl with the stretch marks kneading and smoothing, made concentric circles. She thought of Maureen, her friend, of Maureen's life with men, of Maureen's life in general. Cosmos, where is your order, said the prana in her body. She thought of Maureen's life, and she thought of Steven and his life, Steven doing so well, Steven with his medical secretary, everytime he came home, he looked so refreshed, they never suffered her kind of loneliness, these people. In his mail, came magazines, *Single Life, Come and Get It, Swingers on Skis, Hot Pants Party, Well Being, Carte Blanche Vacations.* They had access, these people, access, access to places, friends, ski slopes, drunken brawls. She could only go . . . where could she go?? To an all-woman's massage workshop, on some decrepit livingroom floor. She was a freak, here among these girls, 40 years old, lying on a Quaker's tiny livingroom floor, getting a free massage, all these girls were twenty years younger than she was! One or two reminded her of Quintana, her pre-pubescent daughter. They were all flat stomached and slim-hipped, wearing size 7 jeans, some looked like they were just about ready for a training bra, so young, so narrow they were, these urban Hiawathas, some did look like Indian boys, and those that had flesh on them, there was one, a gay little girl, she and her friend were making love right on the floor next to her. She was chunky with fleshy arms, narrow hanging breasts that looked like hanging Italian salamis, and a full middle, a substantial rubber tire at her waist, but their flesh, this flesh on the fleshy ones, did not exude a heavy sorrow. On the contrary, the flesh of the fat ones spoke of alternative foods, alternative schools, alternative sex relationships, alternative sex partners, alternative life styles, alternative futures, my God! they had alternatives! The world was opening up for their kind of flesh, but closing on hers, on Gloria's own. Their flesh had buoyancy to it. Yes, it was buoyant flesh, adorned with red peasant skirts or jeans with heavily embroidered red apples, birds, flowers, peace signs, or else "free our sisters, free ourselves" was embroidered on their overalls. The fleshy young gay girl had a red peasant skirt, and a pair of black men's socks, and white fleshy legs with fine black hairs on them. She looked like a peasant out of a Breughel painting, or any old peasant. "I'm not going to let any fucker rip me off anymore," she said. "Is there a room I can go in to meditate in?" said another. "I find that I need the kind of rest you just can't get from sleep alone." "I've just come back from Eucalyptus Hill School in the country," said a third. "Why did you leave?" someone asked her. "Well," she said, and she dove into her world of deep and complicated thoughts, "there's no structure there, it wasn't good for me, the guy who runs it was a Taurus with a house in Capricorn, he was on a Jesus trip, I don't wanna be part of that.

You just can't say to kids... "go do your thing," it's a game you lay on kids to rip them off, you have to offer them something." They all had things to say, these girls. They all had lives and roommates and communal houses they were running away from or running towards. They all knew sex, they all knew love, they all knew getting ripped off, heavy changes, vibes, Continental yogurt and fresh fruit, abdominal breathing, Kundalini and Polar Therapy roommates, Yoga, the Women's Health Collective, the Women's Crisis Center that met each Thursday at the "Y". And here she lay on this tiny livingroom floor with Neil Simon and Judy Collins on the phonograph, belting out their numbers, someone had asked for Ravi Shankar, but they couldn't find him, they said it was such a trip to massage to Indian music, she felt as though she were in the grass alone in summer with summer bugs flying all around her.

"I think we'll save legs for tomorrow, is that all right with everybody?" said Ferne, the massage leader. "Let's see, we've done stomachs , the head and neck, the upper chest and neck, arms, backs . . . I think we're all a little tired."

Gloria asked her massage partner if she'd give her a lift home. "Where do you live?" asked Pat as she dried the cocoa butter off herself, put her hair back in a clip, and put on her ethnic dress with the embroidery. In the car, she was none too talkative.

"I have to hurry back home, this man I used to see called and I have to go home and glue my ear to the phone," she said, smirking.

"Could you drop me off here?" said Gloria. "I don't live here, but I have a friend I'd like to drop in on.

Gloria went into Maureen's house and stuck a large breadknife right through Maureen's upper chest, Maureen was sleeping. Then, warming the leftover cocoa-butter in her hands, she gave her friend the best upper chest and neck massage she knew how, while the blood flowed right out of her. And on the poster in Maureen's bedroom over the bed, the one with the black athletes at the Olympics getting disqualified, (saying "no" to "power"), giving the revolutionary blood-brother salute, she, Gloria, wrote, with a discarded lipstick she found in Maureen's bathroom, her own blood-sister Avon cosmetics haiku, whoever rips me off and my energy off will get theirs, Power to the People! she scribbled, in frosty Nude Again Avon pink, death to all fascists, *death to the fascist-imperialist dogs, death to all male-oriented women, all power to the people, all power to the woman-identified woman, all power to the woman's republic of woman-identified women, power to the people, right on!*

Then, carefully lifting the knife off the floor, she wrapped it around and around and around, using three thicknesses of Scotty Super-Absorbent Paper Towel, put that and the small piece of bloodstained cocoa butter that was left over, carefully in her fluffy pink Fieldcrest bath towel, and headed home on foot. There was not much more to go.

* * *

the unuseable talent

To my jazz greats, Billie, Louis, my Yiddische jazz blacks, my black Jews . . . I am lying here in this bed, I look old. I'm not expecting anything, he's a young man, he has millions of women, he is here in my room, I'm scared, little honeys. I just met him, the day before yesterday, he was painting a house high on a scaffold, a Latino, drinking beer and smoking, the pure Colombian, "my friend, he has the pure Colombian."

He was terribly handsome, with great shoulders and upper arms. His wrists were not bad either, if you like that sort of thing.

"Aren't you afraid you'll lose your balance and fall?" I said.

"No." he says, "I get balanced with Dos Equis and the grass, the pure Colombian, my friend, he has the pure Colombian."

The next thing, he is here in my room. He's here right now, he's gone to the bathroom, and I am here in this bed, waiting for him to come out and come to me in the night, I'm scared, Billie, I'm lying here passive, not expecting anything, why should I expect anything, I'm old, right?? I know he's not that excited by me, oh, he came on very excited, as if he didn't know how old I was, who's kidding who? I am here, naked, with only mildly entertained sexual fantasies now, waiting for the lover to come out of the bathroom and come to me, here he is now, he's coming!

"The water does not go down the sink," he is saying.

"What do you mean?" I say.

"The water does not go down the sink, really, you should go and see, you should go tell your landlady, it is taking too long to go down."

And now, here it comes, the ordinary, the todo ordinario fuck, I wanted the hombre to be thrilled by me, I wanted the hombre to be on fire by my beauty, the captured Spanish maiden, but I see with sadness I cannot be this maiden. So let me at least be the older woman, the non-threatening older woman with her experience and her shriek celebrating the grotesque. I am just going to be ordinary, todo ordinario, he too looks todo ordinario, my Latin lover, he is sticking four ordinary fingers up me, no tight little vagina me, the four ordinary fingers and the sink with the sink water that is taking too long to go down.

Hairs stuck in the sink! Globs of come! Sex without fantasy! I got divorced. I started with lovers.

But how come one day when I'm lying in bed with my book, The Faerie Queene, I hear that you sound replenished by love, Louis, and you, Billie, you sound like you've just dragged yourself home from your chemotherapy treatment. "I'm like an oven/Just cryin for heat/ He treats me awful/ each time that we meet/ It's just unlawful how that boy can cheat/ But I must have that man."

I didn't tell you how I landed in this room, I had three kids and a divorce, and suddenly, I'm alone in a room with a Latino off a scaffold, what do you think about that? When I was married, now that was a situation, I was what they call shut down, not responsive, that's the word, my chakras they were all closed, nailed down, O Billie, do you know what a chakra is?? Billie dear, . . . ("don't you all get too familya . . . whaddya think is comin to town/ you'll never guess who/ lovable, huggable Evelyn Brown, Miss Brown to you") . . . Billie, they were all shut, these chakras of mine, you might say dead . . . but as soon as I got divorced, at age 44 of all things, I opened all of them, all of my chakras, they all flew open at once, chakras one through nine, there's nine of them, I think.

"Why do you let yourself get so thrown?" said my

shrink, the reality oriented one. "These things are just temporary, don't you know? Don't you know people say anything while they're fucking? That's a dangerous game you're playing with yourself!" she said.

Billie, I believed them all! I believed all their crazy words. The words, they lifted me up out of myself, higher and higher, I practically levitated with the words, I believed what any asshole said, I let all these creeps creep in, with all their creepy words.

I was shut down. I was a shut down housewife, is it my fault? I was never open. The chakras they were all sealed shut, and then, at age 44, they all flew open at once, oh, not right away. At first, there was no one. I never fucked at all. And then, it started, the music started , suicidal carpenters, painters on scaffolds, men on unemployment, underemployed men and overemployed men, men of every political persuasion, and especially "the bereftos," what I call "the bereft androgyne," Billie. Step right up! Right this way! A berefto is a man who has lost his confidence. He doesn't have the male prerogative of machismo behind him any longer, so he's vulnerable, he's a female emotionally, powerless and dysfunctional, so to speak, the ones who have fallen off the scaffold, the sad soulmates. The monkey who fell out of the tree.

Now why, you ask, did I even want one of these bereftos? Because there existed the possibility of being totally open with them, it's as simple as that, I wanted a total merger to take place between me and them. They were usually sad, these bereftos, half man, half woman. Okay, I said, gearing up, okay, here it comes, ready or not, a soulmate, a sad soulmate to be sad with, my first berefto, he had a tight little knitted beanie on his head that he had croshayed himself, that's right, they were not afraid of the female occupations. He came to me with his tight little knitted beanie, and he had joints ready rolled inside this hat of his, he always came to my house with an unlimited number of tightly rolled masculine joints, like his tight little balls, oh, he was very sad, my first berefto, he was a young man, very talented, who could not make his way in the world . . .

Getting down, laying back, these were the words. We got down every afternoon at three, with the best grass, sitting on my kitchen floor, the armies of ants trailing under my legs as we sat. Getting down, laying back, crazy words to describe my emotional state. Well, they must teach me something! They must add something to my repertoire, a word, a gesture, an idea, something! I loved these bereft ones, Billie, the androgynes, the indescribably sad male-female ones, the monkeys who fell out of the trees.

Why you sad, dahlink??? I would say, why you sad? O, Billie . . . I was in the throes, streaming.

But one day, I am in bed with my *Faerie Queene,* and I notice that you sound replenished almost never, like your juices have been boiled right out of you (while you're "lettin" 'em!) but you Louis!! shouting, jumping, begging, give me what you alone can give me, a kiss to build a dream on . . . Why, you are lit up like a Xmas tree! Even when you're sad Louis, even when you're black and blue, like your song says, no one ever feels you're breaking.

From a sloth and a sexual sluggard, I became a flaming queene . . . I was a shut down wife. And then I became the flaming menopausal queene.

"Dahling, dahling," they said, "I'll do anything. What do you want? Tell me what you want, right now."

"But I want nothing. I am in Paradise already," I said back.

Then they all disappeared. What did I do/ to be so black and blue, sings Louis . . . Even the psychic I dragged myself to didn't know. She took a few kundalini breaths, that's another word that wasn't around in your time, Billie she centered herself, took a deep breath, closed her eyes . . . "You make a strong heart connection, but I smell stale shit," she said.

I was a Jewish wife. I was definitely not into eros. I was very, how you say? shut down. I tried not to clean and to cook because my mother, she used up her whole life with cleaning and cooking. My house was a pig pen! My husband played around, but what did I care, it seemed so foolish to me, chasing the shiksa the way he did, I just wanted time to read my books. I lay on my bed reading *The Faerie Queene*, but I couldn't even read it, I could never make out what it was about, and listening to you, Louis, with your *Chinatown, My Chinatown!* sweating with happiness, and how you sweat, Louis dear, the sweat of pure happiness, it came through in all your songs, 0 Billie, I knew all your songs too by heart, I could imitate all your phrasing, all your wonderful weird crazy phrasing, that pried the truth out of everything.

Meanwhile, the pages of the calendar kept flying by, just like in those Thirties movies, at least I had time to listen to my records and read my books then, how can a Jewish wife read her books otherwise, time, time, uninterrupted time, you know if the man comes home and interrupts you, it is all impossible, I had more time for my inward journey then, and you know Billie, they sabotage your inward journey if you let 'em, you know if the man is there, he won't let you carry on your inward journey, your "inwardnesse" as Chaucer said, he's too damned jealous. That last Spanish lover I had was so interesting Billie, I wanted to use all my high school Spanish on him, *las palabras*, I said, *mi vida, quiero usar todas las palabras contigo.*

"*Tu eres muy simpatica,*" he said. "What kind of food do you like, chicken? *arroz con pollo?* You like the spices?? ginger and garlic, Chinese food? what is your favorite spice?" he said.

"O, Chinese," I said.

"*Ola!* we will go. We will go and eat together in all the Chinese restaurants, so?? You like the boating, you like the naked beach? We will go, we will go to all . . ."

"*Por supuesto,*" I said. "*Me gusta,* how you say beach, la *playa?*"

"*Sí,*" he said, "*te gusta?* Have you been to the naked beach? Come, we will go, do you like the surfing, you like to rent bicycles in Golden Gate Park? we will go, we will go to all, we will go all over, I will get to know you, all over."

And then it was the four fingers, Billie, four up my toit, and one up my ass, the thumb, and that makes five. And it was still a lousy fuck, because he didn't know about the mind Billie darling, the mind is everything, and they don't know about the mind.

"Oo oo, said my friend Matilda, that fellow really knows what he's about, that fellow really knows about the four fingers, or was it five. oo oo," she said, "the water does not go down the sink, you should go and tell your landlady."

"Of course, yes," I said, "I'm in Paradise right now, don't bother me with questions . . ."

"Goodbye," he said, "I call you tomorrow at seven, you sure you not into mind control?"

"No *niñito, no, soy muy simpatica,* not mind control, I'm in the CIA and I'm going to get Immigration on your ass," I should have said, because he never showed up, he stood me up at the Golden Gate Bicycle Rental!!

"How dare you?" I said, running back to the Golden Gate Bicycle Rental, "how dare you?"

"What you wan', marage? Emotion?" he said.

Oh, these words, these words these foreigners use, they make you swoon, English is so sexy when it's mispronounced, it's not even their words, it's pronunciation, it's their cadence and phrasing Billie, it's these accidental effects of language, Billie dear.

Perfume between the legs, they said, my daughters were all young teenagers, they all left the house with perfume between their legs, birth control pills and loops at 13, stop!

¿A donde vas?

"I'm just going to the park to hear music," they said.

"That's all, to hear music in a park you need perfume between the legs?? This I never heard," I said.

"Don't be so uptight mama," they said, "I'm going to see Gileto, he sings with *Earth, Wind, and Vomit,* he ate me out, but don't get nervous, don't get the wrong idea, he's not your ordinary, rock and roll musician, he didn't only do that to me, open your mind and I'll tell you all about him, that's why I never tell you anything, you're so old fashioned! He's not your ordinary rock and roll musician, he's deep, he's cosmic mama, he ate me out and spoke to me about deep and cosmic things!"

"Cosmic things, is that so, darling daughter? That's very nice, that's a winning combination girlie, he ate you out and spoke to you about deep and cosmic things?" I, the mother said.

Oh, Louis, Oh Billie, these were the words. *Tu eres muy simpatica, la muerte y la suerte*, a kiss to build a dream on, where the lights are low, you sure you not into mind control? *la muerte y la suerte, el dolor de corazon, el dolor de cabeza*. . .

"*Tengo mucha fatiga,*" I said. "Have you lived much? Have you done many things?"

"Toda la corrida!" he said.

"Yes?" I said.

"Si senora, toda la corrida, pues, nada mas," he said.

"But sex, sex is not in the pants," I said.

"Por seguro!"

"Sex, sex, it's in the head, not in the pants," I said.

Before I was married, I was flying off in a thousand directions, Billie. I was putting out for every Tom, Dick and Harry! I said to myself, gee, gee, they really want me. I couldn't believe it, and then there was that time on the train. Now there was a time. How about that time? And the time I went to the little old Italian shoemaker, I was a little kid. A little old Italian shoemaker. My mother thought I was going to the candy store to buy ices. He sat me on his lap and he fingered me, I couldnt have been more than five at the time, and then I used to go there every day, I just sat on his lap and he diddled my clitoris, and you know it was good, and I kept going back. Years later, in my therapy group, they wanted to know why I did it, why, why, why? The whole goddamned world wants to know why, because I felt goddamned privileged, that's why. Because I loved it, that's why, because I was a lonely little girl, that's why. And that's why I demeaned myself, that's why, because someone touched me, someone wanted me, the smug assholes pretended I was depraved or something. He was a little, old Italian shoemaker, that's why. And we went back in that back room of his, he had a curtain back there in the back, that's why. And I was privileged to go back there with him, that's why. Because no one had ever touched me before, that's why. And so I got married.

I got married because I was turning to water or air or a cloud about to float away, I needed an anchor, goddammit, I was fucking everyone! And then came the time on the train, after the time behind the curtain, came the time on the train. I was traveling on a train, it was World War II and there were soldiers on the train. I forget where I was going or what I looked like. I had long hair. I think I wore my hair in a page boy then, I was traveling. The miles were flying by. And there was a soldier sitting next to me, a regular little soldier boy, you know, with his uniform on, the regular way a soldier looks. I am sharing a seat with him, Billie. The next thing I know, he lifts my skirt and he has his dick pressed up against my ass. I just didn't know what to do, there was really nothing to do, he was a soldier and we were both on a train going a million miles an hour traveling to a war, and I was in a suit with my hair in a page boy, it's completely beside the point to ask what I did, you mean did I slap his face or anything? No Billie, I saw no reason to do that. I saw no reason for anything in those days. That little soldier, all he did was take my hand and lead me gently up the aisle to the bathroom, and he fucked me on the toilet seat, and then we walked back to our seats, and the train just kept going, rocking us all into the war and away from the war, I can't recall those times too well, it was just another experience I had. The psychiatrist I had been going to at that time, she said I was so promiscuous before I got married because I was getting back at my mother, always they blame the mother, even though she was a woman, always they say it was the mother that didn't touch you, the mother who showed no concern for you, the mother away in her own dream, well, why the fuck shouldn't my mother be away in her own dream? What did she have waiting for her there with us that made her life such a bowl of ripe, red cherries?

I say shit to that, shit to you, you therapists, doctors and lawyers, . . . we need women's liberation to help us say Shit to you! you professional killers. I've had my experience with doctors too. I had this thing wrong with me when I was married, a yeast infection or a cyst on my ovary, or was it my cervix? Or maybe I just couldn't stand fucking my husband, one of those. And I went to see this gynecologist, a million women had used him, his name was around. After he examined me, I jumped off the table and he caught me in his arms. I was feeling so sad that day, I cried in his arms, and I stroked the collar of his shirt, and then I thought, what am I doing? You're very tender, he said, I could see you'd make a good lover, but did I want that? No Billie, no, I could see he was a pig, he had a thing for women in menopause. "I like women who keep themselves up, women who have preserved their bodies," he said, "I have many opportunities, middle aged women, they come to me just for a little attention, but I don't take advantage of it, I'm too ethical." Imagine him saying a thing like that to me, there I am standing stark naked in his arms, O Billie, I wanted to kill him for insulting me, a pig, seductive and denying it, and I had to hold myself back, because what was in it for me, and he knew it, and he was playing on it, I was so glad to hear I didn't have cancer, I fell off the table right into his arms, the assholes, they think you want their cocks in you, but they don't know, it's their power and money you want.

Tu eres muy simpatica, la muerte y la suerte, Chinatown, My Chinatown, a kiss to build a dream on, where *the lights are low,* you *sure you not into mind control? la muerte y la suerte, el dolor de corazon, el dolor de cabeza, tengo mucha fatiga,* have you lived much? have you done many things?? Toda la corrida! he said, but sex, sex is not in the pants it's in the mind! can you have lived this long without knowing even that? I said.

O Billie, O Louis, how did you come and ruin me with those songs of yours???

"Are you the Jewish wife?" someone asked. First I stopped being able to cook, and then I stopped being able to fuck, or was it the other way around? First I stopped being able to fuck, and then I stopped being able to cook, then it was impossible to do laundry, or make beds, and then I couldn't comb the knots out of my hair, and then I couldn't play the compassion game, and then I couldn't get out of bed to make breakfast for the children, and then I couldn't make the suppers, and then I couldn't talk on the phone, and then I couldn't stop talking on the phone, and then I had knee-lock, and then I had pelvic-lock, and then I became mildly catatonic, and then I shut down, I shut down completely. And then came the divorce, a nice Jewish divorce, with a nice Jewish dike-feminist lawyer, with a lot of graffitti ideology scrawled on her office walls about my right to orgasms.

I was stunned when I went for my divorce. I thought I was supposed to stay married, and bring up the generations, the generations that pass away like leaves, but there

I was in a goyische courtroom in goyische California, my husband had gone ape chasing the blonde shiksa in California, and that's how I stopped being a Jewish wife. When I unloaded that one, I was totally unplugged. I was never into eros when I was married, Billie, what did I know about my right to orgasm? I was just a wife, a Jewish wife yet! I just lay there, and submitted to it.

After the divorce, I slowly started fucking everyone, of course, at first, I couldn't move. I lay in my bed reading *The Faerie Queene,* and the house turned to shit. I mean, it had always been shit, but it got more shitty. Termites swarming in the kitchen, *The Faerie Queene* lay in the bed, my kitchen! Cantaloupe seeds dripping down the sides of a plastic green garbage pail, trails of ants marching bravely in the 3 o'clock sun, I was poor, MediCal and Food Stamps, a half assed broken car with ripped upholstery that gave me exactly three miles to the gallon, teenage daughters all fucking in the bushes, all being eaten out by cosmic musicians, I lay in bed with my *Faerie Queene.*

My youngest child I put in daycare, so I could run to the University to take a degree, I thought I would die if I didn't get out of the house. It was Comparative Literature, my degree. What they were comparing to what, I don't know, for my thesis, I compared *The Faerie Queene* to

Herzog, but I couldn't get a comparison going, so I threw in the bee-poems of Sylvia Plath, along with the short prose of Chekhov. During my oral examinations, one of the examiners said "describe and discuss, discuss and describe."

"So what should I discuss and describe already?" I said.

"Thematic similarities, what else?" the examiner said.

"You mean between *The Faerie Queene* and *Herzog?* Well, let's see, maybe they're both fairies," I said.

"Tell us why you are applying for this degree? said the other examiner, "you know it's a useless degree."

My moronic delivery was beginning to cause a reaction.

I passed those orals with flying colors. I couldn't describe and discuss, discuss and describe, but I managed to say, "Because I am useless, that's why I'm applying for this useless degree." This last minute brainstorm of my uselessness won me top honors, yet.

I've been through it all, Billie darling, the Jewish marriage and the Jewish divorce, the Jewish masters degree in Comparative Literature, a useless degree, and wandering around aimlessly through the wilderness of one night stands, erotic self discovery, sexual shutdown, and Jewish sexual eroticism late in life. From being totally shut down and turned off, I became totally streaming. It was the total streaming of my being, Billie, you know, Lady Day.

After the divorce, I joined the ranks of the newly poor. I got evicted from my house because I couldn't afford the rent, but I found a rich aesthetic person's house to housesit for a few months. My lover! We had many rendezvous there, hanging plants and statuary, dripping fountains, candlelight, paintings, Oriental rugs. I drenched all those expensive Oriental rugs with all the fluids of my being. Streamings! When I lifted my shoe off the floor to put it on, a gush of streaming poured right out of my shoe. This I have never seen before, the lover said, "is it pee?" *"No, señor, no es pee-pee,* it's because you're such a good tongue man, a great sash and trim man, you give good head, I said, Eric Satie on the $19K sound system and you give good head," I said.

I fucked them all, Billie darling, laid back carpenters and potters, painters on scaffolds, men on unemployment, dropouts of every political persuasion, and most of all, my specialty, "the bereft androgyne." Soulmates we will be together, I said, what a connection! After my first love affair with my laidback potter, the filthy kitchen floor every afternoon at three, children's yellow school busses farting up the hill, trails of ants marching along in the blazing 3 o'clock sun, regular platoons. After I left him, I found a sculptor who couldn't sculpt anymore, "nobody's doing anything worthwhile," he said, "it's all self-expression, not art, self-expression is therapy AIN'T ART," he said, "this 2000 year development has reached its zenith, and nobody knows where to go from here, I'd rather do something honest like play pool or eat candy bars."

There I was, falling for the words again! Another bereft one, fallen into classlessness, orbiting the outer rim. But when I asked for those new orbits, when I cried out, to be fed, to be fed. "I'm burned out," he said, when I called on the phone, requesting chats of dailiness, believing of course in the weirdness of ordinary life, he had to run, his meatball was on fire, or he had to go soak his bicycle chain. "Gotta go polish my shoes now, gotta go listen to old Jack Benny programs on the radio, gotta go pick out my hanky for tomorrow, gotta go eat my Hershey Bar with Almonds, I've been saving it for eight o'clock tonight."

So ended the myth of the soulmate-bereft-androgyne, the soulmate girlfriend, only with a prick. Whatta laugh! They were just as inaccessible as your ordinary man, these bereftos, the same withdrawal, only more so. So what did all my streamings do for me, Billie, what????

After that, I took the classic nosedive, when it was all over with the sculptor, when the regime of the bereft androgynes had come to an end, I nosedived out. What I have now is the psychic healer, to hell with psychiatrists, I say, it was just an unuseable talent anyway.

"Imagine a pipe," she says, "the top comes out of the center of your head, the other end, somewhere halfway between your vagina and your asshole, now, Breathe! Fill your chest and abdomen with air, and slowly, slowly, let the air come down that pipe, slowly, slowly, between your asshole and your vagina, let it out! the universal breath, love yourself, she says. You see that picture on the mantel over there? That's my guru, love yourself, he says, you gotta love yourself, even if it kills you!! O Billie, and now they're asking me to love myself, why are you and Louis singing those songs of yours if we can all love ourselves so much? Now, Breathe! My guru is a big exhibitionist, he does it with mirrors, Breathe!"

First, I knew nothing about my hungry heart, Louis, and then I began my responsive phase, I couldn't wait to get with a man to try out my responsive phase. I could drench a 12 by 15 Oriental rug with all my streamings. Eric Satie in the background, we were naked on expensive Oriental rugs. I gave wonderful little rectal kisses, I had a special way of washing balls and assholes with soapy little washcloths, "Why don't you have cards made up?" my friend Matilda asked, very discrete, with a phone #: "Asshole Kisses and Eric Satie".

"What you wan' Marage? Emotion?"

So now I an in my psychic's livingroom. I have just had the healing massage, and she is giving me a cup of strong French Roast coffee before I go home. I am asking who is that old man in the picture on the mantel over there, is it a father? an uncle, a *Zeyda* maybe? No, she is saying, that is my guru, he has some very interesting ideas.

Ideas? I am saying. "I thought we did not do ideas here."

My guru says you gotta learn to hang out with yourself, she says, that's the biggest idea.

Step right up, I'm barking in front of the carnival tent. Right this way! Failed men of all sorts. Failed husbands. Failed painters. Failed actors, failed poets. Men with the wormy realization you can maintain a relationship with nobody, I will fuck you all.

And now I have experienced transports, Billie, (*Miss Brown to You*), transports that come with humiliation, I know I will be left and uncared for. I have learned to open myself only to find that I am about to receive the electric shock of total humiliation. One day, one day Billie, I lay in the love embrace. I notice I am spreading my legs very wide, I never even knew they could spread that wide before, and I see that all I ever wanted was to open to everything, to death and life, and the Prince of Darkness who comes to my livingroom every night. . . . *"are you the one who wants to open to everything?"* he says, *"are you the one dying to open to it all . . . ?"*

. . . the man thinks I'm opening to him, but I'm really opening to my own despair, the jerks think we're doing it for them, can you imagine such a misunderstanding? My sculptor said I was using sex for the wrong reasons, you use sex for catharsis, he said, would anyone ever dare say that to you Louis dear? Would they tell you you had become a geek of sex, to be put in a cage on display at a zoo?

There I was. My transports fuck scared away my sculptor, and my tiny little fuck that means nothing, my little zen fuck, my todo ordinario fuck scared away my housepainter. My little no ego fuck, my nothing fuck, my letdown fuck, it even startled me! After those Cecil B. DeMille fucks, I entered the phase of my blah nothing special fucks, that's right, *blah blah, todo ordinario.* To the little Latin housepainter, I tried to explain it. *Todo*

Ordinario, I said, trying to teach him illuminated zen fucking. *Vamos a ver, todo ordinario,* (asshole!) he never came back, it was nuance wasted on the lower classes.

So I retreated back to Cecil B. De Mille. Swept away, by blood and sand. *Du sang, du mort, et du volupté.* I knew nothing about any of these fine points when I was married. I myself got so scared by *Todo Ordinario* that I flew back into *El Spectacular* when it was really ordinariness I wanted.

First I was a Jewish wife, with no response. Knock. Knock. *(Are you the Jewish wife? they said.)* Then, when I became totally responsive, I learned I had no value on the meat market. I couldn't trade in on my sexiness, it only made me more of a stray. If only I could hear them from a oneway mirror, the ones I gave transports to are saying . . . she's too desperate, and the other ones, the todo ordinario ones are shouting . . . that I'm too much of a bore. The more I discovered my sexiness, the more I found I was Lear in the storm, besmirched, befouled, *"bakoked".* "You use sex for the wrong reasons," said the sculptor. *"You use sex for catharsis!"* and he promptly ran. To my scaffold painter I cried out . . . 'Stop grabbing me. Don't be a grabber.'

"Sex is subtle. It's all up here!" pointing to his head, I said.

"You sure you not into mind control?" he said.

"Todo Ordinario," I said.

"You will teach me, teach me. You have experience. Teach me, help me. Help me with my English. And teach me sex. You have experience. You finich??"

Rhyming with spinach.

"Todo ordinario," I said. And then, he left, forever.

And now, I have come to the end of the line. Last week, my psychic put her hand upon my heart.

"What happened to you? Your heart is frozen."

Ha! Ha! I cackled, ha, ha!

Ho ho, ho ho!

No

One

Wants

Me

Anymore

Ha ha, ha ha, ha ha,

Strange fruit now, Billie darling

Now I've discovered the power of sex,

I'm cremated

Cremated bowels for the unlikely

Connoisseur of fucking

(say goodbye to mommy / say goodbye to daddy)

"*Regardez,*" I said. "*De la muerte. Del sangre. Del corazón. Todo ordinario. Tu eres muy simpática,* these were the words."

You into mind control? You finich? Rhyming with spinach? You using sex again, for the wrong reasons? You using sex for catharsis? A kiss to build a dream on? With a man in a restaurant? Is that all you really want?

No, I said NO, "*Sophisticated Lady*", I drenched all those Oriental rugs with all my streamings, with all the fluids of my being, and I developed my natural responsiveness, only to have it be one more unuseable talent. And that's why, that's why, . . . "*when nobody is nigh,*" *I cry.*

* * *

notes from the tower of menopause

My name is Ursula. I am an absurdist. Let them stick selfhood up their ass. Let them stick a room of your own and selfhood up their ass. Or any combination of the above up their ass. He wrote me a letter and it sounded like this:

Dear Ursula,

What I'm writing about is Outcomes and Intentions, we've had a Rotten Outcome, haven't we? Now, in order to have a good Outcome, there must be a clear Intention, w/no Distraction. First, people have to be up front, so they can be clear about their Intention, maybe here is the core, maybe you've never been able to be up front w/me.

I've told you what I want, I want my family, the kids and you, you without your resentment and hate. I'm not quite sure what you want, have you ever told me? Have you ever stated it? Are you even capable of formulating an Intention? Whenever I ask you directly, you play some funny game, you say, "why don't you take the initiative?" What kind of an answer is that

Ursula, think, think, what can I conclude from that? Besides, your asking me to take the initiative, isn't that so unlike you, isn't that a retrograde position, totally out of line with your other retrograde positions?

All I can think of is that coming from your present attitude towards me, my taking the initiative would just be a joke from such a committed "ballbreaker". Darling, I love you, you know I love you, I have always loved you . . . suppose you are being honest, why won't you state your Intention, why won't you reveal your thought process to me? Intention Times Distraction Equals Outcome, that's the formula, work with me, work with me Ursula, you have to take some responsibility in describing what kind of relationship you want with me.

I found it agonizing to hurt you by telling you about Sheri the other day, and my asking her to move in with me. On the other hand, for 18 years now, you've been rejecting me, so why should you be surprised or even hurt that this should happen. The fucking truth is Ursula, that I'm in great pain right now, I need your help, either help me by releasing me so I can go on my way to set up a life for myself, or help me by clarifying your position, so I can move towards you, move towards you or get the hell away.

You've got to beef up your Intention quest, darling. Intention is not the result of a warm emotion or impulse of the mo-

ment, it's the result of a lot of blood, sweat, and tears. I know this is hard for both of us to do, we've both been living without this sort of rigor for most of our brief lives. I can't believe you planned it this way, you're not that crafty, impulsive, yes, malicious maybe, but I don't think you had it in you to deliberately lie about wanting me, even wolves have their honor, right?

You've got to ask yourself, do you really want a relationship with me, period. No female soup of Distraction, it's time to stop playing ingenue and be a real grownup, it's time, Ursula. I have warm feelings for you. And hate too, the hate however is only superficial. All I have to do is hurt you a little, and the hate feelings dissolve and the warm ones come pouring out. But I'm not so sure about you, sometimes, I think your hate runs so deep that ain't nothin' gonna get them out, is that true??

Help Ursula, help me, I feel like I'm dying. I've ALWAYS LOVED YOU, DID YOU LOVE ME? Let's both step out of this bears-trap of a a situation.

Love forever,
Minsk

Intention. Outcome. The Female Soup of Distraction. I must be an absurdist, none of this makes any sense to me. A Brooklyn absurdist like Henry Miller. I love Henry Miller, he's a Brooklyn absurdist, also. I'll give him

The Female Soup of Distraction, he's moved in a Sheri into his apartment and he's crying to me about relationship with me??? I say, shove it up your ass, asshole, that's right, take your most cherished ideas, . . . Relationship! I'll show him relationship! . . . He wants what I couldn't give him in the first place. Last night I got a letter, the fiftieth night letter from him in a row, I need your help, I need your help! That's all I hear, I need your help! I don't want a man who's asking for my help, why don't you give it to him already, Anna said, tell him you'll give him 12 minutes of help the first month, and a total of an hour and twenty minutes the first year, make it contractual. Contractual, she says, she's another one! All I wanna do is sit on my bed, reading Krishnamurti. Then I wanna run with the boyfriend. Then back in bed with myself sorting all the night letters. I don't want a steady diet of anyone thing. You name it, the answer is NO! What does he want when he says either move closer to me or, or what? I know that he knows he can't move closer to anyone. So he puts it on me! This dreadful inability to move closer to anyone, ha! Give of myself? We have no self to give of! Relationships are dead, open marriage, closed marriage, it is all absurd. No one can move any closer than they are already. To anyone. That is just another bullshit story to take your mind off the fact that you're going to die. It's time to go now. I have to meet my lover, thank God Minsk went back to Santa Barbara. The lover wants me to put the kids in *The Son of Frankenstein* movie today so we can talk seriously for a change. Now, what serious thing do we have to talk about? Furthermore, you should be withdrawn from relationships for awhile already, Anna said, feeling the way you do, she's another one! You'd think, she said yesterday, you'd think you'd just want to take some time off from relationships to cool out. Are you kidding? Aunt Sisy got married five times after the age of 60, I reminded her. Boredom sends me. Boredom with myself sends me to men. Boredom with men sends me back into bed with Krishnamurti. Boredom with lovers plunges me into bed away from lovers and into myself. But soon I get bored with that. That honeymoon ends quick. There is no resting place for me anywhere. I have no home. I run from one to the other out of boredom yes, boredom sends me. But each is more boring to me than the one before. The husband sends me to the lover. The lover sends me to bed with Krishnamurti, Krishnamurti sends me to myself. Selfhood. Lovers. Husbands. Books. I have no illusion of selfhood. No illusion of life with husbands or lovers. Krishnamurti tells me to find my quiet center. My husband tells me to shit or get off the pot. My lover tells me I'm ripping him off not taking him seriously as a person. My self tells me I'm nothing. It's really quite a bore. I can't stand this women's movement that tells me I have a soul, that I should off the man and go into my own soul, into the room of my own. The old straight world tells me I should find happiness with husband, children, lovers, or any combination of the above. They lie. They all lie. They can all stick selfhood up their ass. Let them all stick Molly and Me and Baby Makes Three up their ass.

    I don't look my age. I put the Swedish Blonde in my hair. My lover told me I had a skinny back, a skinny child's back. He was surprised to find I had such a skinny child's back. The husband in Santa Barbara I can't divorce. He calls me twice a day. He wants me to shit or get off the pot. Shit or get off the pot, he says. He's always loved me, he says. Did you love me, he wanted to know. Don't shit me about love. Maybe I'm stupid. Maybe I'm angry. I know hunger. I know taking a shit. I don't know no love. In the hospital, when they wanted to change my sheet, I told him to wait outside the room. Delgado wants me to think about that, its' very fundamental. A man offers you his arm and you tell him to wait outside the room. If he loves me so much, how come I feel so ripped off, how come

I feel so put down? Something's fishy. He says he's loved me all these years, why haven't I been standing behind him? I don't wanna stand behind anybody! I wanna be in front. And I don't wanna get divorced either. What do I do if I get divorced at age 46? He's moved in a Sheri. He says he needs more than an empty apartment? He needs a woman there with him? Shit or get off the pot. You just have a bad script, you're just working out your mother's hate for your father. I know you really love me, You're just in the grip of repeating your mother's hate script for your father. I'm 46, what's in it for me to get divorced now? The wave of divorcing is over. Is there something great I'm gonna do? Will I write a great collection of poems like Anna? Or go to Social Work School like Phyllis? It's too late for social work school. What's the advantage in getting a divorce now? This way, I have a roof over my head. I have someone to fight with. I have someone to spend Thanksgiving with and Passover. The aggrieved lover came over. After the husband left town, the aggrieved lover appeared.

"I feel very ripped off by you. I took you seriously as a person. I listened to you. But you only toyed with me." Don't be silly," I said. "What was there to take seriously?" If I had put any pressure on you for a serious commitment, you would have run away from me fast. He started to cry, a six foot six man stood in my livingroom and cried real tears. What are you crying about? I said. You have a wife, a child, a child with asthma yet, can you imagine? What did you want me to do? I said. The last lover ran away because I wanted him to marry me, and this one is crying because I'm not taking him seriously as a person. Why should I get a divorce? Is there some big advantage in it for me that I don't see? Who will support me, a woman with no skills, the erstwhile beauty with the erstwhile good tits and ass. It's not as though I have some hot alternative. Delgado says, think, think about it. Here is a man who after all loves you, the father of your children. Then why has he moved in a Sheri into his apartment? Why do I feel so bad? What will I have to run to if I think I'm bad off now? Phyllis has some dopey job as a paramedical. Anna believes in her ability to invent a new vocabulary of the emotions. I believe in nothing. Phyllis is paramedical. Even Sheri is some kinda paralegal. I am a para in nothing. Why divorce him now? At least I have someone who makes long distance calls to me from Santa Barbara. I have no myth of talent. I have no interest. I have no compulsion to work. I met Joe Wasser. He left his wife and kids because he had a compulsion to write. When you lose the compulsion, you can forget it kid, you can hang it up. He was right. I told him all about me, how I felt. Do you always talk like this? He couldn't believe it. You've got such a great head. Is this your normal way of talking? Sure, I'm a philosophy queen. What else? What do you expect, it's only my life. I talk for my life.

You're a writer! Nobody should talk like this and not put it down on paper. Everybody tells me that. I know, I told him, "I've got a Mexican straw basket at home full of my writings. They all sound depressingly boring. I've been home with that Mexican basket for four days now, sorting. What a migraine it gave me. Nobody will help me sort this shit, nobody." I begged Anna. "You've got to sort your own shit," she said. Delgado is no help. You're going along each day, bobbing up and down. Bobbing along being a creative liver. I could never do that he said. I worked hard to get where I am, well, so did I, smart ass, can I help it if the world gives him structure, money and appreciation and I get shit? He's very bad on the Woman Question, you get an F Delgado on the Woman Question. My children, my husband, they annoy me. Take the burden. Be a regular person. If I have five good minutes a day with my wife, I'm ahead. What does Minsk want anyway, a family?? A loving supportive relationship with you? Normal desires, perfectly normal desires. Wait a minute, I say. Where's my praxis? Where's my life? My children annoy me. Minsk disgusts me. Help me out of this. Teach me to live with boredom and despair. Ambiguity and frustration. Hand me the burden. The burden of being human. Let me live with the boredom and frustration like a regular person. Move closer to me or move away so I am free to get someone else. Help, he cries. Help me. Either move closer or move away. A regular family-life. An Open Marriage. Or free me to be with Sheri. How unseemly. Free me. Help me. Move into my space. And help me. How can I help him? How can I move into his space? I can't even move into my own. This Minsk has got be kidding! And yet he's not threatening me. I must be serving some purpose for him. I am sorry to say that I am serving the purpose of a game. His stuckness with me is just a diversionary tactic. He'd rather play anguish with me than face the fact that he's fifty and going to die soon. So he talks relationship. What is this relationship they are all talking about? Relationship to yourself or another. They are both a lie. You can't have a room with someone and you can't have a room of your own. There is no other and there is no self. Look at you, I told Anna, you got divorced and you ran to yourself. I can't get divorced because there is no self to run to. I have no illusion of selfhood. I have no illusion of me, myself, and I. Love is dead and self is dead too. Goodbye selfhood. Who is this Delgado, my Med-i-Cal shrink, he wants me out on the marketplace. I could never just live, like you, he says, you just jump in your car and move around. I could never bob along each day like you. Take the burden. Be a regular person. Get out and work. Life is frustration. Life is not dreams. Work as a waitress in an ice cream parlor if you have no skills. Or work as a cleaning lady and clean people's houses, anything! Don't cry to me about fulfillment. and praxis. Just get out there and be with the living. But those night letters. Do you know how many night letters I've had from him in a row? Five hundred at least, analyzing my script. Telling me he loves me. That he's pained when he hurts me. He's jacking off with sorrow! Help him, he says? Well, fuck that, I'm not going to enter his space and help him. Who's helping me? Togetherness? Shit or get off the pot? He must be kidding, I am his game. Let him look to himself.

I want a man that doesn't ask for my help. Understand him? Support him? Emotional support? What a bore. What a big baby! Relationships, you say? You don't have to pull that shit with me, I'm reading Krishnamurti. People come to him with problems. Hate, lust, aimlessness, despair. He always tells them the same thing. Find quiet inside yourself. I'll give that Minsk relationship! I'll torture him first. I'll give him a run for his money. I am an absurdist. A Brooklyn absurdist. Like Henry Miller, a Brooklyn absurdist. Let them stick selfhood up their ass, I'm not even an absurdist, that's too high class for me. Then came this lousy hysterectomy. Why me? I'm not the kind of lady that needs one of those. The growth in the uterus, it was very large, larger than most. You could feel it from the outside, just by putting your hand on my stomach. It felt like a baby-sized kosher salami. When I found out I had it, I went to visit Minsk in Santa Barbara. I tried to laugh with him about it. Look, I'm getting so strong, I'm growing a muscle in my stomach. I went to laugh with the lover too. The lover with the sailboat and the ex-wife. And the child with asthma. We would go out onto the bay and make love there. We lay in the cabin and made love. My wasp man, he's allright, a nice, middle-aged man. A divorced man, my nowhere man, my wasp lover with a sailboat. I'm tired of Jewish men. All they do is talk. The intellectuals. This one at least had a sailboat. It has its advantages. You can go out on the water and make love there. Here, feel this new salami I have growing in me. It's my new muscle. That ain't no muscle lady. Go to a doctor! He too had had experience with wives. Two wives prior had had ailments. Isn't that what wives do? he said. Aren't wives there to remind us of ailments? If you were my wife, those doctors said, I would take it out immediately. They too needed wives to remind them of ailments. If you were my wife, I'd take it out today, but you're not my wife, so go home and think about it. You've got six months to think. So? I took myself home to think about it. You know what? There was not that much to think about. However, I was so used to thinking in the category of useless things, I thought about it anyway. One of the things I thought about was can we dissolve this by chemical means. I lay on my studio couch wrapped in my fifty foot telephone cord calling up doctors. We can give you hormones to make it grow bigger, but we can't give you hormones to dissolve it. So I had the hysterectomy. I was lucky I had no complication. Delgado came to see me in the hospital. How come you're so depressed about leaving this hospital? Why don't you want to go home? he said. As if he didn't know already! I don't have praxis, Delgado, what do I have to go home to? It's easy for you to talk! I have no praxis in my life at home. You, you are a fine one, you have somewhere to go everyday, and people to see, and you have just bought yourself a red red rug and a Danish chair besides.

I saw them in his office, he couldn't hide them from me! It's not that easy for me, Delgado, 46 and no praxis, and a hysterectomy, I have no people I see. I practice nothing. And they pay you money yet! So stop being such a smart ass and asking me how come I'm depressed. I have no home to go home to, and if you don't know that yet, you're even jerkier than I thought you were, and I thought you were pretty jerky to begin with, what do you say to that Delgado, what smart answer do you have for me now? Ha ha! I'm going skiing. I won't be in the office next week, he said. That's what you get for having praxis. You get the red Oriental rug, you get somewhere to go everyday, and you get to go skiing to take you away from all your difficult praxis. I lay in the hospital room cursing everyone, cursing my lack of praxis. Until the Cookie Monster came on from Sesame Street.

    A week later, I got home. Minsk was going to lunch with friends. Can I go along? I begged. I bent over and put on my fishnet hose, incision or not. I had just been catheterized two days before because I couldn't pee, but two days later, I bent over and put on my fishnet panty hose to see what lunch was all about. Lunch was a black cavern of despair. I came back from lunch knowing I would never yearn for it again. I came back home and got into bed with two codeine and two perkadin and swore off lunch forever. Will someone please look in my Mexican basket and tell me who I am? My recent reading includes Wittgenstein *On Certainty*, Simone Weill on *The Need for Roots*, Simone de Beauvoir on *Aging*, Sartre's *La Nausée*, Alan Wheelis on *How People Change*, Shakespeare's *Tempest*, Chekhov's *Short Stories* (the Penguin Edition), Dostoevsky's *Idiot*, Susan Sontag, *Against Interpretation*, Fritz Perls *In and Out of the Garbage Can*, and Krishnamurti on the still silent center within you. I have them all on the floor by my bed with my Mexican basket, tangled up with a very long telephone cord. I know I'm a poet, I just can't stand the work, cookie, my ego is too weak to impose a form.

While we were at lunch, I met a nice poet man. He wasn't at our table, he was with someone else,

"What do you do?" he asked me.

"What do you mean, what do I do? I've just had a hysterectomy."

"No. Not you." He couldn't believe it.

"That just goes to show how little you know about everything," I told him.

I came home and got into bed with two codeine and two perkadin.

"I'll see you sometime," said the poet. "come back and talk to me. I'm always here."

"I'll never see you again, let's face it. I'm never eating lunch again."

All the people at lunch had praxis, where's mine, I said to no one in particular. I was the only one at the table who had no praxis. Even Sartre said you get out of la Nausée with a little praxis. But I had found none. Minsk hadn't either. He tried to blame me, and I tried to blame him, but let's face it, both of us went through this life without ever finding it. I begged Anna to read his night-thoughts. I found them in his Mexican basket. Please read it, I said to her, then you will understand a very immature person. But she wouldn't read it, she said she has enough trouble with her own night-thoughts. Yea, but hers don't say, "I can't fuck my wife because she reminds me of my mother." You don't have those kinds of night-thoughts I told her. A Danish chair and a red red rug. And someone to pay him sixty dollars an hour. Delgado is an ass. I told him I was switching to someone else. "Why?" he said.

"Because you're a drip."

"Don't switch. You've got to learn how to relate to the drippy side of yourself."

"You're too much of a drip. I need somebody sexy." He wasn't doing a thing for me. Sixty dollars an hour. Delgado is an ass.

"Go out and clean people's houses. That too is praxis. Go get a job in an ice-cream parlor."

So that was the end of that year, 46 and still no praxis.

"What have you stuck with in all these years?" said the new psychiatrist, Yancey, the sexy one.

"The children."

"That doesn't count," he said.

Whatta jerk! I got them all on tape. All the ladies crying. And all the shrinks telling me to live. Wonderful tapes, if only I could make a play out of them. My poetry, it's nothing, it has no form, no ego to impose a form.

"I've done all my scripts," I said. "And I'm tired of them all. I did charming. I did sensitive. I did intelligent. I did potential. I did suicide. I did depression. I did sensuality. I did wife. I did the middle-aged birth of the self. And now, I'm doing stuck. Unstuck me, please."

"I don't have magic," he said. "Here we have words. Here we talk. You talk. I listen. Me, Tarzan. You, Jane."

He was really something, that Yancey. Whatta turn on! He had virility. Delgado is a sad sack by comparison. His ear looks all shriveled with sad stories that have been poured in there. Yancey was handsome. He wore tight pants and cowboy boots, the shirt open at the throat, exposing the pulsing, phallic neck. I was up for a full half hour after I left his office.

* * *

your thing is sticking out p.s.

When my friend Goldie offered to introduce me to Fats the Buddhist, I was excited. She had gone through a lot, was a nonstop-talker. I was trying to write some interviews, and needed fresh material.

"Won't you come in, this is my kitchen," she said, "everything here is plastic, do you like it? I'm trying to write an article for the NY Times Magazine Section, do you think there's a literary mafia, somebody I know told me they just throw it out the window if you send them your writing and they don't know you, do you know about that?"

"What can I say?" I said.

"I'm awfully naive," she said.

"There probably is a literary mafia," I said, "mafias are everywhere, how could there not be one there? p.s. I heard you used to be crazy once, but now, you're better."

"I never have been crazy, just miserable, and now all this weight from all this medication. Have you ever heard of psychiatric assault? I've just come back from meditating in a retreat in Santa Cruz, I'm a Buddhist now, I wanna be treated like a Buddhist now, I'm so tired of that Zen look, the media, they ruin everything, everything good they come and ruin, now I love plastic, the truth has swung the other way, plastic is the truth now, it's a pleasure living without ferns for a change, if I see another hanging fern, I'll hang myself. Here, it's all plastic cups and plastic spoons, plastic dishes, everything from the Blue Chip Meditation Center, or is it the Blue Chip Stamp Redemption Center, you'll have to excuse me, you lose all sense of everything when you've been meditating for two weeks straight like I have, but it's much better than being crazy, that's for sure. I've become the Buddhist, can I get you some coffee? I've gained a lot of weight, how about a cereal beverage? That's what they drank in the retreat, herbal tea or a cereal beverage, Lillian my roommate, she inherited a whole trunk full of Blue Chip Stamps."

"Where'd you get that dress?" I said.

"You mean this? It's just a sheet from Value Village. Here's my scrapbook. Have a look."

"It's probably true. There probably is a literary mafia, mafias are everywhere, how could there not be one there?"

"All my works are in that scrapbook. I'm a Buddhist now, up from Welfare and into Buddhism. Out of the crazy house and into Buddhism. Down with spiritual materialism. Down with psychiatric assault. I guess there is a literary mafia. YOU seem upset, what's the matter?" she said.

" I think your dress is not quite pulled down over your knees."

"I don't pull my dress down over my knees anymore. I let it all hang out now that I'm a Buddhist."

"But your private parts are sticking out, I think I see your private parts, what's that thing??"

"I'm a Buddhist now. Here's a show I had out in Laguna Beach in 1957," she said.

"But pardon me . . . I see your thing. Your thing. How can you expect me to look at your portfolio when your thing is staring me in the face like that?"

"Here's my entire scrapbook. You can see for yourself that I did entire moon landings in 1953, way before the government space project was launched. All my shows are covered here in this scrapbook. I was doing moon landings and moon surfaces long before they ever had a space program."

"Pardon me, I'm having difficulty concentrating, it's my head, do you have an aspirin?"

"I've learned not to take every sensation so seriously,"

she said.

"That may be easy for you, but I . . ."

"It took me 50 years to learn to tune things out. It was awful. I had to become a Buddhist to accomplish that."

"A super-terrestrial being with super-terrestrial intelligence has just walked into the room, and it's sitting under your dress, grinning at me," I said.

"I'll get you the aspirin, although I don't believe in medication," she said. "Of course, how could there not be mafias? Of course they throw your writing out the window if you're not one of them, mafias are everywhere, here I am in 1956, they wore suits then, the Civic Union is giving me a gold medal in this one, this is a write-up I had in the Santa Monica Screech Owl."

"O my God, your fat beefy, I want it, I don't need it, but I want it, can I have it now?"

"This was from my show in Los Altos, 'Fat Housewife Turns to Moon for Inspiration', it says."

"But your fat-beefy, it's listening to our conversation, It's squashed but amused down there."

* * *

"The retreat was great, I needed to get away, I'm into healing now. I'm . . . into the high energies now," she said.

"Please don't pass out, . . . no es necesario, Buddhists know you don't have to have a nervous breakdown over things. You find out when you meditate, there's no need to escalate."

"Everything was fine until I saw it, why did you show it to me? Was it an accident?"

"It showed itself," she said. "I changed my name from Rita to Fatso, you can call me Fatty. I needed to get out into something. I was married. Now, I'm 49, see me at my birthday party, here, these pictures. All the kids are here, all these kids, 21, 22, 23 year olds. Baropa Nyngama's wife is over there, she's the one in the purple velvet, he's considered a saint, all these Buddhists at my birthday party, you wouldn't know it looking at me, would you? You might think I was just a fat, crazy housewife in Safeway, buying eggs, is it? Or scouring powder, I don't look like one of the beautiful people, but come see my work, then you'll see me. I have painted and painted. I have pained and pained. Come look at my scrapbook. I have two paintings hanging right now, guess where? In the Outer Space Division of the Smithsonian Institute. Paintings of the moon, of man's or woman's first trips on the moon. I painted these from my head long ago, long before anything like the man-in-moon space project was launched in Washington.

I was a housewife. My husband was in Public Relations. He made a good living, I forgot what you call a good living, Buddhists don't pay attention to things like that. I suppose he made as good a living as any, silly the way people call things isn't it? I don't understand it, I got married young, and sex was never good. I knew I should never have gotten married. My mother said he was a very acceptable man, very presentable. I tried to change my mind at the last minute. I knew, I had a feeling it would be no good. We never even went to bed, in those days, you didn't, you had to be very pure then. But I knew somehow it would be no good. I went to my mother and I said 'I can't go through with it,' but she said 'the invitations are printed up already,' people don't do things like that, give it a chance, and I had to go through with it. But that's my mother. My mother has been the source of problems my whole life, even my shrink says so, but the Buddhists don't say things like that, they talk about karma, it's more interesting, I don't really know if any of it is true. It's all a point of view. Everything's only a point of view, and there's millions of them. The shrink just says what she has to say, and the Buddhists say what they have to say.

There I was, married with two kids. Before I turned around, they were gone. The boy is studying to be a millionaire. No, excuse me, he's studying meditation in a commune in Colorado, and the girl, her career is splitting up with husbands.

"But is the boy studying to be a millionaire, or . . . meditation?"

"A small difference, don't let minor things bother you. Let's say the boy is studying meditation, and the girl, she's entranced with breaking up with husbands. She lives on an island off Washington, has a one year old baby girl. I sure don't feel like a grandmother. The kids like to see me when I'm fine, when I'm fun to be with. I can do everything they do. I can drop acid and smoke dope, and meditate, and just go on all the trips they go on, but when I'm in trouble, that's another matter, then they don't want to be near me, then I'm disturbing their peace and serenity, then they can't meditate or something. I've accepted it, it's all right. But now I'm really having trouble, do you want to hear? It'll help your book, we're just two crazy people writing a book, aren't we? because the troubles I'm in are just what you're writing about, women's troubles. We could write a Hollywood script about it and make a lot of money, then it would be worth it at least.

It's like this. There's this guy I'm friendly with. He's black and very spiritual. He fasts four days out of every week, he's a Meher Baba person, I don't know. He's into a lot of things, but he's very nice and everything. He said he wants me to meet his mother. I don't wanna meet your mother, I told him, I'm older than your mother, I'd feel very funny. Anyway, I was sleeping with him before, but now I'm not into that anymore, for the time being. I just wanna see where I am and get my head straight. Anyway, he thinks I'm very spiritual. I showed him my paintings and he couldn't believe it, and he brought his brother over and his brother's girlfriend, and they liked my paintings very much too. They couldn't believe it either. And they said they wanted to sell some of them for me, and they took two away and they were very excited. Anyway, then I have another problem, I thought this lawyer was going to be my agent, he said he wanted 25%, and I went to see him, he lives up in Tilden Park, behind the Rose Gardens. There was something I didn't like about him, I don't know, but then I asked around, and I found out 25% isn't that high, but, somebody is still checking up on that for me. Do you know anything about the percent an agent gets? Anyway, then my roommate, she's been very depressed lately. She met this guy and she was very excited about him, he's been this hobo for 25 years, and he has a lot of stories and Grove Press wants to publish some or all of his reminiscences, but he can't spell!! He knows about life, but he can't spell, and he asked me and Lillian would we be willing to type up his manuscript, he called up last night at 12 o'clock. I had fallen asleep. I was feeling very crazy because there's this guy who comes to my window every night now. I was getting undressed with the curtains open, I was just laying on my bed, and I see this person in the window, so I went and shut the shade. I was alone in the house, and I said, go away, just go away, but he wouldn't, he just was in the window looking at me with a funny expression on his face, and I got very scared, I didn't know whether to call the police, eventually I did, but he was gone by then, and it was just horrible, the police said, "we know you go to the bar next door, we've been watching you, and you know you should keep your shades down." Apparently, they must know something about me, but I don't know what, because I go to the bar next door? Well, my house is right next door to the bar next door, so I hang out there, it's mainly a gay bar anyway, and my landlady came and said the same thing, she said, "you don't seem to understand that you're not supposed to go to the bar next door."

I need someplace to go to relax sometimes, I said, most of the people are gay and crusing there anyway. Anyway, now this guy comes to my window every night, last night he came again, but Lillian was so upset, I didn't know what to do, and Slackey he was supposed to call, and I wanted to call the police because how can anybody live like that, but Ruth, that's another friend of mine, she said Lillian was in too bad a shape and it would hurt her further to call the police, You know what pigs they are, the last time we called them, they said we had no business going to the bar and getting a reputation, I had no idea I was the cause of so much attention. Do you think it's wrong of me to sit in a bar and relax in the evening? But something must be going on, because I went to this lawyer on this deal I have, Oh, don't ask, it was a terrible deal with a silver mine and I lost $15,000 on it, and I wanted to see him also because I'm thinking of working on the Alger Hiss book again, and he was going to be my agent and even he said to me . . . What's going on in that house of yours? What's going on in that house of yours next door to the bar? Evidently somebody must've said something to him because he made some reference to sitting at the Red Hippo and getting a reputation. I don't know what people think, I mean, till the age of 40, I never had any sex life at all, I was just married, and my husband didn't know how to screw and I knew even less, I just painted all these weird pictures of the moon and men in outer space, thinking really of women in outer space the whole time, and now the word is out that we're running a whore house here or something. I don't know what I did, I just went to the bar a few nights to relax, and it's even a gay bar! There aren't even any men I bring home or anything, but that doesn't stop anyone from talking, I guess they think the gay bar is a setup or something, and that I'm doing my business and it doesn't seem obvious, there are a few gay women around there also, but I don't know, I must be old fashioned, I'm drawn to women, but I never had love affairs with them. And tomorrow my mother is coming and I'm gonna have to go to Seattle with her on a Greyhound Bus, imagine spending 21 hours on a bus with your mother! This lawyer, I decided I don't wanna, he wants to take 25%, and he's not even a literary agent. I just get into these things, I'm too goodhearted, I leave myself wide open and then people rip me off, I don't understand, but the alternative is even worse, the alternative of being so straight and so uptight and just sitting on your own little egg all the time. You have to have people, I know that, but if you're open, and open your trips to them and want to know their trips, something doesn't work out right there either. And now with this crazy guy coming to my window every night at four in the morning, I'm gonna have to get out, Lillian is sick of me, she says she can't live in the house, it's just a crash pad. I just had one or two parties and then Mojabi came, Mojabi who is named after the Mojabi Desert, and wanted to stay, she had no place to stay so she was staying with us, and she didn't have any money. She was very nice giving us back rubs and everything as a gift in return for staying, she gives wonderful back rubs, but then she started taking my clothes and using my bathtowel and my toothbrush even, and just taking everything she wanted. I'd like her to stay, but really, even my bathtowel! The back rubs were nice though, she was such a pretty girl, just came out of nowhere with her pretty smile and backrubs and no bathtowel. Anyway, I can't talk too long today, I'm on my way to two places. First, I have to go return this Astronomy book to Laney College, I signed up for an astronomy course but the instructor wants to give a quiz at the start of each period and I can't do that, I took the course because I get ideas from these pictures, look at these pictures, did you ever see such beautiful pictures?? This is the kind of stuff I paint. I showed you my scrapbook and my slides so you know. But I can't take a 20 minute quiz every day, that's not what I'm there for. It's a $35 book, I'd like to keep it because I get ideas from it, but $35! So I thought I'd return it first, and then I have to go to the Welfare Department. My Med-i-Cal hasn't come through yet, and I need to go to Dr. Pose . . . he sees me when I need him, I have to get a prescription from him for librium, but I need the Med-i-Cal to go get the prescription. So I don't know what to do first. Maybe I should keep the book already . . . . . $35 but it's really a good book, and you can't see pictures like this just anywhere. Maybe I'll keep it already. I can sit with it while I wait in the Welfare Department, they'll think I'm crazy sitting there with colored pictures of the moon waiting for my worker to waltz out with her weird costume. I don't even know who my worker is, so I'll have to wait all day probably, they ask you who your worker is when you come in, and if you don't know, they can't put your name down in anyone's book. And then you really have to wait all day. So I might as well have some good reading.

The thing with my mother is really bothering me, she knows I have no money, but she thinks I'm a baby and can't handle the money in my trust fund, she has a trust fund for me, but all the money is tied up. First, my son said he would take care of it for me. And then he invested in this silver mine that fell through and now he says I shouldn't bother him, he's busy meditating, and I'm trying to manipulate him to make him feel responsible for me, but it was my money, and he was the one who lost the $15,000. My daughter is another one with her one year old baby and her divorce. Can you imagine? I'm a grandmother now, but I feel like the grandchild . . . don't tell anybody that one. Maybe I'll tell the Welfare Department I expect them to play the role of my grandmother, or the lawyer who was supposed to act as my agent who I now have to drop because he was robbing me blind, imagine asking for 25%, he knows I've got my finger on something, he must know something with this Hiss book, I showed him the manuscript and he said I must be a genius to have figured all that out by myself, but it didn't take much figuring, I was just there at the trial in 1952, I had a seat and sat through it and took notes. I know that book is something, it's really weird when I work on it, the typewriter drops on the floor or the paper flies out the window, something weird always happens, and then I've got the other book, the one on Dostoevsky's mistress, the first modern woman, now, there was a woman, she ran away, she went to the University, she was the first woman in the University, she wrote, she kept a journal, letters, she was fighting for her life. I know I have a good book in that one, and in the Alger Hiss book too, the question is who will be my literary agent. I was all set to have lunch with Hiss in New York way back when, we had the date and everything, and then . . . he was suddenly called away or something, it's all weird, everything surrounding that book . . . that Slackey, he really hurt my feelings. I was just sleeping and minding my own business . . . it's not my fault if you have to walk through my bedroom to use the bathroom, he just came through in the middle of the night and I said . . . who's there? who's there? . . . "it's me, it's me," he said, "I have to use the bathroom," so I didn't think anything of it. And then, after he used it, he had to pass through my bedroom again, Lillian was in bed waiting for him, so he came over to my bed and he said . . . "Oh?" "That's all, just . . . "oh?" Oh, you've got a waterbed, I always liked water beds, but I never had one, can I rest here with you a minute? "All right, I said, I guess so." And before I knew it, he was making love to me.

"Well, how did it feel?" he says. "How did it feel?"

"It felt fine, how should it feel? Love is love. But then in the morning, he wouldn't say a word to me, maybe he thinks I'm gonna tell Lillian or something, I don't know – he told me he had very little to do with women, he said he was a hobo all these years, for 25 years he's been a hobo, or 30, something like that, but the way it looks, in two days, he's had two women, and I don't know how many others there are. I don't know if Lillian's mad at me, if he told her or she guessed, I just don't know what, but she's really acting weird slamming doors, she said the house had no peace in it, she had to meditate and do her trips and all, but what did I do? I just had two parties and then Mojabi named after the Mojabi desert came and asked to live, and then as far as the Red Hippo next door, it was only a place, what else could it have been, it was just a place to hang out and relax, so it's really very far-fetched that they thought I was a whore. Like I said, I lived without sex for the first 40 years of my life, and now everyone thinks all I want to do is get in bed with people. If you can give me a lift to the Welfare Department, I'll go wait for my worker with my astronomy book. I think I'll just have to find a spiritual commune to live in, these cheap apartments with people in the window and gay bars next door don't seem to be for me, and the extra room we always have to rent to lower the rent and somebody with no bathtowel of her own always staying in the extra room. Besides, the Welfare Department thinks I'm paying too high a rent to qualify for SSI, I don't really know what they think I should have to pay, we're already splitting $180 three ways, well, we had planned to, but right now Lillian and I split it in half, and then who but Mojabi, you know, but if she wasn't there, we would try to get somebody else who could share the rent. I don't know what's gonna happen with that SSI. Dr. Pose said he wrote them a good letter about me and that I should get it, but they turned it down and I appealed, and he wrote another letter, and this time, he said he's sure I'll get it. So I'm waiting to hear from them and I'll have to pack up everything and vacate that apartment. I thought it was going to be so good when I first moved in out of that Halfway House, imagine, a 49 year old woman in a Halfway House, but who knew about men coming in through windows, and girls who appear out of nowhere offering massages with no bathtowel? And now Lillian is slamming doors telling me I've destroyed her peace of mind, and I think she is silently accusing me of stealing Slackey. Really, I didn't. Like I said, the apartment is laid out so you have to cross my bedroom if you want to use the john in the middle of the night. And then he was really heavy. He rolled over on me and I heard a noise and I got very worried because I thought it was the waterbed and he said, "did I break your waterbed? and I said "no, no, I don't think so."

No no, I don't think so, that's what I'm always telling them, good little girl that I am. (Hey Joe whadya know? I just got back from Mexico. You are a shmo But please don't go No, no. I don't think so.) I thought it was just one of the watery noises of making love, I mean, he seemed to know how to do it, but then again, I'm not sure. Even though I'm 49, and you'd think I'd know, I really don't know a thing about sex, does anybody? Anyway, next morning, wouldn't you know it, the bed had sprung a leak, he did break it, jumping all over me like a billygoat . . . and I was up from 5 a.m. on, shoveling water down around the floor on my hands and knees, and he was sleeping in the next room with Lillian. It was really something, he just seemed to have sex with me on the way to the bathroom, I was just part of taking a pee, well, you never know, sex is different these days, when you think of all these 20 year old girls having hundreds of sex relationships by the time they're 22, so much for roommates and apartments, I'll just have to find a spiritual community to live in, Maraga Kngthu has something on Dwight Way, and Caring Love, try Caring Love, they say, there's a good scene for middle aged women there.

A friend of a friend, she has a tumor in her breast and cancer all over her body, but she takes off all her clothes with the 19 and 20 year olds and celebrates, singing and dancing in a circle with the unmarred, beautiful ones, girls with long hair and visions coming out of their eyes, and it is something, she has one breast, the other, a botched up scar where the other breast used to be, waiting to die, she eats lentil pie, Tuesdays and Thursdays, with blended tea, honey and water, with the best of them, kicking her feet in the air, she's dancing, she's laughing, with the colostomy bag flapping! But I will have to find myself a spiritual commune, where else can a 49 year old woman live, and pay the rent, and maintain a waterbed without a leak, and keep the windows free of faces? I'll do that after I get back from the World's Fair with my mother, four generations we'll be, four generations, my mother, me, my daughter, and her one year old baby girl. But now, I can't talk anymore, I've gotta go return this $35 book, maybe I should keep it already, the pictures are irreplaceable, I could use this for some sketches, funny, I saw all this in my soul without ever seeing a scientific picture, I painted pictures like this 20 years ago, 10 years before any mention of going to the moon, I just looked into my soul, and I saw all these "surfaces," of the moon they were, all these places in outer space. Just like the Buddhists say, the Buddhists have finally come to America, and am I glad! How did they ever get so smart?? Well, why do you think I became one?

So now it's . . . 'going, going, gone', I'm off to see the Wizard (the wonderful wizard of Oz) *the curtain descends, everything ends, too soon, too soon* . . . I'm nuts for Cole Porter, I can't wait to see my worker's outfit, such a meshugena dresser.

"p.s. But your thing is sticking out."

"So what's so terrible? If it wants to stick out, let it. No one understands Buddhist clothes, they have a mind of their own, no? I think I'll keep the book already, $35, but at least I'll have something to read in the Welfare Office."

* * *

the small revelation

o what can ail thee, knight at arms?/alone and palely loitering . . .

Mega *was* alone and palely loitering, but even she didn't know the half of it, she just walked around, as usual, older, yes, lost and sad. Every night in her dreams, she was tied down to the railroad tracks, woke at 3 am, just as the train got her, and made some cocoa in the kitchen. What was it? She certainly didn't know, and no one else did, not the g.y.n. she went to see, complaining of insomnia, not the female internist, who said her blood pressure had to come down in a month, or else she'd need a calcium channel blocker, so she joined a Group. Although the young ones in Group saw her as an old woman, (what was she doing here?) Mega continued coming to Group and sitting there zombie-like, the oldest member. It worked this way, there were four men and four women, and there were two hours to "work" in. You took a piece of chalk that was lying on a blackboard ledge, and you wrote your name on the board if you wanted to "work". Work, work, work, just like what she had always done, but had she ever worked, the Group wanted to know, was what she had done in her real life, bringing up children, was that "work"?

She hardly ever "worked", she just sat, dazed, stupefied, with a peculiar affect the kids in Group pretended not to notice.

(so . . . what can ail thee, knight at arms?)

She was tall and gaunt, with exceedingly dry skin, the pedal pushers she wore were vintage 1948 or 1950, though it was now 1974. She sat on the floor with crossed legs just like these young kids, in the half lotus pose, on early spring evenings, trying to be like them. Really though, she had bottomed out and didn't give a good gooddamn. But if only her knees could cross like theirs, if only she could sit and listen, if only she could "work," asking for strokes, asking for pleasure, staying in her "adult."

The g.y.n. had put her on an anti-depressant, elavil, but she was a zombie here, wrapped in bandages, she watched them, glassy eyed, and they seemed to nod at her. Every Wednesday, she came back, but she never "worked", it was the young kids who worked, didn't they have lives to live, problems to solve, happiness to find? The young Sally, should she be in love with that guy driving her crazy . . . Tim, who was mad for her, Sally who came to Group and said, "I had an awful weekend last weekend, I visited my mother in her country house and I felt like making an apple pie, but by mother said, "we don't have the ingredients."

"Your mother was 'pigging' you because she's jealous of your beauty," said Narcissus Navajo, leader of Group. And then we all analyzed her script, the child, the parent, and the adult. "Stay in your adult, and try the world of love," said the co-leader, Élan, and "take risks, and get strokes" (negative strokes are better than no strokes at all) and "sort out your child, your parent, and your adult," and "Sally has the right to love whomever she wants, how she wants, when she wants." Once the leader of Group, Narcissus Navajo, a man trying desperately to look younger than his actual age, said to Sally, "you're an exceptionally beautiful young woman," and she was, she had the moist golden brown skin, creamy and silky, and long brushed thick light brown hair that fell over her creamy shoulders, a California girl, and she sat there, very disturbed about pigging herself, "I pigged myself an awful lot this week," she said, sitting there with her long Picasso-Saltambique legs, California golden as well, the perfect elongated bones, exquisitely formed toes, a foot fetishist's B.J. (blow job) fantasy.

"1 had a terrible week, I really had a very heavy week this week, pigging myself, my pig was really on me this week," she said, and then came the story about Tim putting pressure on her to love him back the way he loved her, or how her mother wouldn't let her make the apple pie, then came the story of the threesome, a man named Dr. Shepard and his lady, they had invited her to be a third, they were breaking up their insidious formation of "a couple" and needed a third, and she was it, except now, she realized she was being used.

"Wonderful!" said Narcissus Navajo, the inspired male leader, a man who wore very tight shirts and Navajo jewelry.

"Right on! said Élan, a woman grateful for the chance to be trained by Navajo, the chance of a lifetime, genius of the interpersonal.

"Taking care of #1!" said Group, us poor saps all paying $140 a month, lending support from our avowedly shaken support systems.

"Offing the couple," as a bourgeois and toxic reality, was the "in" thing of that week. Sally's way of working out was asking for what she wanted, not what anyone expected of her, Tim included. The pie and the mother story was a clear example of the "pig parent", Sally had mastered Group Talk and Group-think, and right now, Narcissus Navajo was giving her feedback. "you're a very beautiful young woman, righteously disturbed, earnest and willing to work, taking risks, asking for pleasure, exposing yourself."

Mega just sat there staring, with her long lumpy legs, her ill-fitting, mildewed pedal pushers, the dry, wrinkled skin, the ravaged zombie stare, glass-eyed, damaged, never working, never "exposing" herself, never taking "risks," never saying a word, never even writing her name down on the board. Inert and silent, sitting, just as down as the week before, no change, why was she coming to Group? the leader asked, Narcissus Navajo.

"I'll get to it," said Mega, with her zombie shrug.

Gradually it came out, like a painful pee, Mega had an ex-husband, she was in process of getting divorced. Her children were big and grown. She had lived with husband Sam in the mountains for 30 years, unplayful years, very much mummy years. "Why so many years?" demanded Narcissus. His bracelets shook, Narcissus Navajo of the tight-fitting body shirts, and the silver Navajo jewelry, they were very fancy bracelets, he was into adorning himself,

In Berkeley's Green and Pleasant Land   194

giving vent to his "female" side. And of course, he had found a lovely way to make money, people were waiting in line to get into his groups. "Why did YOU allow yourself to stay so many years?" he demanded.

Sometimes, Group would try to draw Mega out, they would say she looked better . . . "You're looking much better than last week," they said, "have you started that swim class at the "Y" yet?" or,

"what's going on?" they wanted to know.

"Oh nothing," said Mega.

What had she done that week?

"Oh, I've just made some drapes," or, "I'm painting the walls."

Then we would all go round and give her "support" and tell her how much we liked her.

"I like you because of the way you sit, you keep your back straight when you sit, under all the bandages, the mummy (you) looks warm, I like you because of the great pedal pushers you wear, I really dig the color of your socks, I like you because so much seems to be going on inside you, and your way of working is so silent, because you have the composure to not laugh easily, I like your seriousness, I like your dead seriousness, the seriousness of your socks, I like you because you always wear socks that never go with the color of your pedalpushers, I like your socks, I

don't like your socks, I like your shoes, I like you, I don't know you but I like you anyway, you're a closed tomb, but so what? and those socks you wear, they're groovy colors, and they don't match, I like you, I like you, I don't like you because you're old, but I'm 'workin' on it, I think you're disgusting, you've wasted your life, but your socks, your shoelaces, green and unmanageable, I like you because I imagine you sleep in men's pajamas, you look like the kind that sleeps in men's pajamas if someone gave you a pair, or gave you half a chance, I like you because your nose doesn't interfere with your eyes, the way some people's do, I like you for wearing red sneakers, it shows something about you . . ."

That was "feedback," that was "strokes." And there was Mega, collecting them.

And there was Group, feeling guilty for hating her and not giving a damn. There was Sally, reporting on the pies her mother couldn't let her make. There was Mega, wrapped in bandages, a wounded silence.

One day, Narcissus worked on Mega even though she didn't put her name on the board, he said it would be much better for her to give up the elavil, Group would help her "cope."

Then other things happened, and others. Mega came

to Group, got off elavil, said she was doing fine.

"Fine, did you say "fine?" said Narcissus.

"What do you want to do?" said Group, "you have to want something, otherwise you're not in the game."

"I used to swim . . ." says Mega.

"Wonderful!" says the co-leader, Élan, nodding to the bad-boy genius Navajo, "what a beautiful, exceptional young woman you are, Sally!" he is saying.

"You, where could you swim?" says Élan, warning Narcissus with her eyes to pay attention.

For two more Wednesdays, Mega returns to Group and just sits, death again. She doesn't put her name on the board, everyone is listening to Sally's tales, her rippling, sexy voice, full of waterfalls glistening, her white wonderful teeth cavorting, a playful dolphin, diving for sperm in the sun, her latest chapter in the toxicity of couples, or, its counterpart, the toxicity of threesomes. Élan catches Mega on the way out of Group . . . "How're you making it without the elavil?"

"Oh, fine, I guess," says Mega, she is smiling slowly, doing her mummy shrug.

Then, one Wednesday, Mega comes and says she's found the "Y".

"Wonderful," says Group, "far out!" and Group turns

to listen to Sally again.

Mega sits tight for awhile, attending, while the others work on their pig. When she starts working again, she speaks about the people she lives with, Navajo thinks she's putting herself in a very disadvantaged position, staying with friends, he's struggling to give her attention.

"It's all right," she says, "that'll stop soon."

Then Group asks what she wants to do again, how could she fill up her time.

"I think I'd like to draw," she says. "I was always interested in drawing the thirty years I was married to Sam in the mountains. I always thought I was interested in drawing."

"What could you do to facilitate that?" says Élan.

Mega ends up taking one class in drawing from a live model, and one class in botany, she always loved leaves casting shadows. Next time she comes to Group, Group tells her to keep a notebook on class interaction, and when she finds it difficult to talk in class.

Meanwhile Sally continues to glisten and gleam, diving deep for sperm. By this time, she has given up on the hopeless affair with Tim, who had to leave the state, he was so love-crazy, and the threesome relationship is a bust as well. However, there is a new relationship starting up with Bob, the bearded young graduate student in Group, who sits across from Sally every Wednesday, staring at her open legs. He has said that his wife is not as sensual as he needs a woman to be, Group now watches Bob looking longingly at Sally, we are witness to the pained yearning coming out of the cautious and decent Bob, the troubled, festering gray heat coming out of the shy graduate student. We all sit on the edge of our cushions. Navajo especially gets a bang out of it, beautiful Sally and this poor tentative Bob, who only wants someone to rub him with strawberry yogurt when he gets home at night, and eat it off his penis.

"I want someone to lick it off my dick," he says, when Group asks him "what is your fantasy?" and Bob, the frightened, tentative graduate student, with the tenspeed bike, who likes hiking and biking, and studying and loving, and knowing how to show everyone how he is not a victim of machismo, but is instead a sweet, affectionate male says, "I want someone to rub strawberry yogurt on me and then I want them to lick it off my whole body, especially my dick."

"With a tireless tongue?" asks Navajo Man.

"With a tireless tongue," says Bob.

Then Group gives him strokes for risking, for asking for pleasure.

Mega sits. Then one day she talks about a man in Bolinas, who she goes to see once every two weeks, because she needs "strokes," she is using the language of Group now, but he is not her kind of man, she says, somebody from the past, because there is nobody else. "I'm gonna stop it soon," she says, "it really doesn't satisfy me."

Now she sits quietly in Group again, another couple of weeks.

Everyone's very satisfied with her progress now, she's swimming, she's taking a botany class and one drawing class, she's keeping a notebook on why she can't talk in class. One day, several Wednesdays later, she comes to Group and looks very depressed. "why don't you work tonight?" someone asks.

"Because I have nothing I wanna work on," she says. Well then, ask for something from Group. "I think I wanna Group massage," she says. "Sure! Far out!" Élan: "That's a right on request," at least she's asking for things(!)

Mega proceeds to get down on the floor, the dead cells lie down on the imitation Oriental rug, all the hanging ferns are testifying, "which side do you want first?" super bright and eager Élan. "I'll lie on my stomach, Mega says, "all right, you have 10 minutes," says Navajo, glancing at Group clock. Mega hides her face in her elbows, so no one can see her, Group can all see the familiar pedal pushers, the familiar light blue Ship and Shore blouse hanging out of the pedalpushers, and the sneakers. "Take off your shoes," some one says, "and we'll massage your feet." She unties the laces of her large sneakers, my god, they are boats!! and she lays her face down, hiding from her cruelly distorted feet. Navajo Man, our leader, looking at the clock again, says "okay, 10 minutes," Group gets down on the floor all around Mega, all except Navajo, he remains seated, immobilized, frozen in non-participation, genius of the interpersonal.

Group, we all rub her back through her blouse, a brave soul rubs her ass through her pants, another pair of hands pulls at her lumpy calves. Someone gets down with knuckles on her feet.

She didn't know which hands belonged to which faces, and she uttered a phony moan. Go ahead, moan, moan, release! screams Élan, but that is the first and only moan we hear. Then the 10 minutes are up and everyone gets back up off the floor, in nightmare choreography, we all go back to our cushions. Mega, she stays for a few seconds on the floor, face down in the rug, her nose sniffing at the dust. Everyone is trying not to stare, but we can't help it, her image is tantalizing, a sign charged with signs, an old woman, hiding her need, and ashamed.

"That was very good," she says, getting up, the color in her face a shade lighter. She sits back down in her seat, "that was good, I needed that."

No one sees her face in Group for the next two or three weeks. One Wednesday, someone says "what happened to Mega?" She called, says Navajo, she's staying out to celebrate her daughter's birthday, and next week, she's celebrating her own. You mean she has a birthday? We gasped, no one could understand why she would want to celebrate that disaster; three weeks later, she comes back and sits in her old seat in her old way again. "How old were you on your birthday?" asks Navajo.

"Fifty."

"Fifty? I never dreamed you were as young as that, you look much older."

* * * *

That was the last time she ever came to Group, but I missed her, I had been older than most of the other people also, and I had things to say to her, so I phoned and went to see her.

She was lying on her couch when I walked in,

Thelonius Monk was on the sound. She had gotten her own place though, she had taken Navajo Man's advice after all, on a table near her, there was a copy of *Let's Get Well* dumped in an ashtray, and used dental floss.

What kind of man was your husband?? I asked.

"Oh, Sam, it's funny, when we lived in Pasos Verdes, I went to a psychologist, and he said to me one day, "you know your husband Sam is not such a sensitive man, as a matter of fact, he never developed beyond the age of two." But I never really let him say anything bad about Sam, I always protected him, it's weird, I gave my whole life to him."

"I've had my life," she said.

What did he look like? was he exceptionally charming, or what?

Oh no, he was just ordinary, I don't know why I used it all up on him. The pictures of Sam looked very ordinary to me, a bald guy in a T-shirt, with an oar in hand, in some kind of rowboat, like a million guys with bald heads and T-shirt and oars.

He had me believing he was a genius, she said.

Well, was he?

He was smart. He was a CEO. And he never let me forget it. But he was often boring. I saw it coming.

What did you see? I said.

One day, he said to me, "You have to start getting your own life together now." Who would have guessed?

As we talked, neighbors filtered into the room, a young stewardess from next door, then an old psychiatric social worker Mega was altering a skirt for. The psychiatric social worker took off all her clothes and walked around in her opaque panty hose, something out of Genet, no bra, panty hose, and a hat with a veil. Mega showed me a few more pictures in the family album, Jim-Jim, the son, up in Alaska, commercial fishing, standing in a boat, holding a big fish, Luisa, the daughter, at a party, the only Caucasian among Asians, "she's getting a Ph.D. in Far Eastern Studies at Radcliffe, her subject, Religious Festivals of the Far East."

"I feel sorry for Jim-Jim, his father never gave him recognition as a man," she said.

"Yes, I was thinking for awhile Group had nothing for me, only I never told this to Navajo, instead I told him I was sick, my son is a con artist, he can con anyone out of anything, but his father conned him out of his wife, can you believe it? My husband ran off with his only son's wife. Group never knew this about me. Why, I'm practically a Greek myth!"

What was her problem? I said.

"Susanna?" She was the oldest of 16 children on a farm, she had to take care of all the other children. She had a lot of chores, she was always attracted to older men with money. She's enthusiastic and blonde and has a lot of energy, and she's into Transcendental Meditation, Gurdgieff and walking barefoot on hot coals. She loves spending money and she loves buying clothes . . . Sam must love that too, the boy wrote his father saying he forgave him, he wanted to see him again, but Sam wrote back and said he was busy. Navajo knew for awhile I was suicidal, once he went round the room and asked . . . "how long do you want to live?" when it came my turn, I said , "I don't know, till I'm 65, I guess . . ."

"That's funny, I want to live as long as I can," he said.

He still didn't understand why I was so wiped out, but I said to myself, 10 or 15 more years of this life, why, it's more than I can bear.

Seeing the daughter with the sensitive face and seeing the son who could con anybody out of anything, but most of all, seeing the husband Sam in the rowboat with oar in hand, squinty and bald, sporting the plaid flannel shirt, that was a small revelation, but of what?

"You know," she said.

"No, what??"

"Look, one day Navajo wanted us to do some homework. Go home and think what you want written on your tombstone, he said, and who you want at your funeral, and what you want them to say about you, and then report back to Group. I went home, cleaned the house all week, thinking all the time, and then I quit Group, don't ask me why, I finally understood something, damned if I know. But you know Navajo, how he makes it tough for people to leave? Calls it resistance, and all that crap? So I told him it was the age thing. He thought about it, very serious, *"well, yes," he said, "there is a little of that, I can see what you mean, there's something to it, there's something to the charge of ageism."* At least, he didn't deny it. Mega laughed, jiggling imaginary Navajo bracelets.

"I thought Group was very ageist," I said, "strokes were reserved for Sally, how I resented that girl!"

"I rather liked her," says Mega, "she was a brave girl."

* * *

she had mastered the art

Since she had freed herself from the nastiness of marriage, she had mastered the art of appearing as if she had had a life of heavy experiences. I have lived, her being sighed as she entered rooms. I have lived and you don't know the half of it. She had mastered this pose much as a kabuki dancer with her chalk-white face.

The week before, she had had a disturbing dream. She dreamed she had a baby, but it didn't have a baby's face. It looked like an old man's face, maybe Nehru's . . . somebody like that. She was still married to el creepo in the dream, and she had to go shopping for something, so she left the baby with him. There were other people in the house too, but nobody paid attention to her. Nobody said, "wow, you had a baby! That's terrific!"

Nobody said anything.

The baby was weird because it wasn't acting like a baby and she wasn't acting like a mommy to it either. When she got back from shopping, el creepo said he gave the baby a haircut. She thought this was odd because the baby was only two days old, and she didn't remember that two day old babies got a haircut.

"Why did you give the baby a haircut, you're not supposed to give a two day old baby a haircut," she said to her husband.

"And I fed it too," he said.

"What did you feed it?" she said.

"I fed it Snackpack."

"Snackpack? That's crap. You're not supposed to feed a baby Snackpack. It needs special food."

Then she started screaming.

She was telling this dream to her current boyfriend, Ed, who seemed to be listening, but she wasn't sure. As a matter of fact, his listening was a little off, flat, dry, hostile, certainly the wrong kind.

"I felt they were all playing dumb on my time. Like you," she said. "You're not listening to me either."

"How about if we go to bed now?" said Ed.

"You know, you're a real ass, and a macho ass at that. Nobody's real except you, that's it, isn't it? My god, how long have you been like this?"

"What did I do?" said Ed.

"In the dream, I start screaming, and I can't stop. 'Well,

this must be the post partum fit I had congratulated myself on not having,' I say to myself. Then I go back to look for el creepo to chew him out some more. I open the door and there he is, in another room, a bathroom, and three men are shaving in there, singing "ole king cole was a merry ol' soul," and there is a young girl, maybe 15 or 21 sitting on the toilet in a brown and orange sweater with her head in her elbows, all anguishing and sobbing. Nobody pays attention to anybody. The men act as if they don't know the girl is there, and nobody knew I was there, and when I leave the bathroom, I realize we are all on a train speeding across whole continents, over vast territorial nonentities . . . while men shave, singing idiotic ditties, and girls sit on toilets, crying."

"What do you think the dream means?" said macho man.

"I don't know. I think I've lost control of time, I mean, the train is speeding," she said.

"Sounds to me like you've lost control of more than time," said Ed.

"You're right, I think I've lost control of everything."

"Come to bed," said Ed.

Then and there she decided to dye her hair for some reason.

Bill's Drugs was quiet on this slow Sunday at 3 in the afternoon. She often did this on a Sunday, browse through cosmetic departments to help pass a draggy weekend, she always liked to buy new eyeshadow or a new lipstick, or a cream rinse for her hair. She picked up a tester lipstick and tried it on, not bad, at least she was out of the bright killing sunlight. And tonight she had a date with Ed, even though he was a selfish ass. She would take home the ashbrown Miss Clairol, put it on, clean the house while it was changing the color of her hair, and then she'd be ready for her early evening out with Ed. Only a man for Sunday evenings before the work week began, only a man. With soft ashbrown hair and painted nails, she would play receptive, she could pretend she was there with them, listening intently, she liked the pose, it was kabuki art. If she looked beautiful, any ugly scene between a man and a woman could be orchestrated. It was the best game of hide and seek, she was hiding and nobody was seeking, it had a terrific ambiance, or was it anomie. Depressing, but necessary, somehow or other, anomie had become her addiction. She needed to be alone in this way, this was her meditation, this was the way she did it best, not by really being alone, and not by being with a woman friend, a woman with her chatter and her psychologizing and her longterm depression and her conversation loaded down with futile yearnings. She loved more than anything else looking good on Sunday evenings, with soft ashbrown hair, matching nails and lipstick, a soft angora and lamb's wool sweater, a man to take you out to a heavy flick with you looking gorgeous. Her strong suit was gorgeous hair and cynical talk about the poison and the power struggle of relationships. You could only do it looking good, if you were looking downtrodden, depressed, debilitated and dysfunctional, you couldn't get the sharp edge of that sexy anomie, you couldn't get the ambiance of a destroyed ambiance that was the heart of her style. She was still beautiful, only half destroyed, not totally.

In a few hours, she would be sitting somewhere with Ed, but anyone would do, any man that took her out on a Sunday evening, tossing her well-styled hair, laughing broadly and fully with the middle-aged teeth that were still somehow baby white, the gums red as a dolls. I will not age, she had promised herself, my hair won't gray or brittle, my hips won't fatten, my teeth won't stain. She continued to appear year after year as a woman not of 45, but as someone of indeterminate age who had had too many love affairs and was hung over from jamming too much into her life.

"You are a terrible conformist," said Ed, " a self-styled female outsider who also wants all of the ordinary emotional female experiences. This is what I hate about you most, that you dare to combine Simone Weil with Betty Grable, you are a conformist to the nth degree, so much the worse for you that you try to appear a non-conformist."

So the great Sunday evening had fallen flat. All that search for the right hair rinse and that freshly butchered ambiance. She got into bed without flossing her teeth, how could she meditate twice a day when she couldn't even floss her teeth once? And she stared into the curtains covering the windows, down into the dust of it, the dusty warp and woof of it all. She knew she was used up without having really been used. She had been unused really, but she had carried off the game of looking used. She had mastered the art of appearing to have used, but she cried with the knowledge of her indistinct and puny aptitude for life.

* * *

the mother's wasteland

After she fed me the tea and smelly cheese, she asked whether I wanted pickled herring. Then she said, "I'm not ready to paint yet, do you mind if I sketch you first?"

In my mind, I admired the makeshift aspect of her studio. "I like your room," I said, "it looks like an artist's room"

"It looks like a poor artist's room," she said.

"How did you get that rubbed-out look on your piano? . . . Now, that's something."

"You just sand the paint off, then you paint it white, then you rub around a little with a rag."

"I love the rubbed-out look," I said.

"You are the perverse one, aren't you? In love with entropy, or is it decay?"

The trees blew outside her window, so many trees for the city, it felt country-ish.

"Are you sure you're not bored to death, just sitting there?"

"No," I said.

Just sitting there with nothing to do, watching a pool of sunlight on her bedspread, trying to consolidate my losses, I kept sitting, she kept sketching. "Tell me about your marriages, how many marriages have you had?" I said.

"An ungodly number! Three," she said. "I had *three* marriages, isn't that a shameful number? God knows, I have tried that thing!" And she laughed her aristocratic laugh.

"Tell me about husband number one," I said.

"Husband number one . . . I was very young. I didn't know a thing when I married husband number one. Are you sure you're not getting bored to death sitting here?"

"Oh no. Tell me about husband number one."

"I was a child. I didn't know a thing."

"Tell me anyway, I want to hear," I said.

"Well, I was 20, and he was 22, and it was love and sex, and that was husband number one."

"What happened then?" I said.

"Nothing happened, silly. Who said anything happens?" And she went on sketching my head.

"I'm getting your head now," she said. "You really are a patient one, aren't you?"

"It's very soothing. Will I be able to have this painting when you're done?"

"We'll see," she said.

"Tell me about husband number two," I said.

"Well, husband number two. Husband number one wasn't an artist, he didn't know anything. He was very nice all right, but he didn't know a thing, he didn't know a thing about the imaginative life. And then I met husband number two. And he was an artist, poor Mr. Crouton. As a matter of fact, he was the one who told me I could paint."

"What happened then?" I said.

"Whoever said anything happened," and she laughed the aristocratic laugh again.

"We got married, and we had a child, and the child was beautiful, and I stopped painting because I felt I had to support that child, my husband felt he just wanted to paint pictures, and the child was an imposition on him, he didn't want to support a child, don't be silly."

"So you went out and supported the child?"

"Of course. The child had to eat, didn't it?"

"And then what happened?"

"You're always asking 'what happened'. Isn't there another approach to things? What happened was that eventually husband number two didn't want to have any sex at all, and I was very horny, so I went out and found myself several lovers."

"Didn't number two mind?" I said.

"Of course he minded. But I minded not getting fucked, and husband number two was very hurt and went on painting pictures and not fucking, and I went on having my lovers because I was very beautiful, men liked me and I liked men."

"That figures, you're still quite the beauty," I said.

"Do you really think so? I was beautiful once, that I was for sure, but look what happens to the skin, the skin sags so and the eyes close, and the color goes out of everything."

"No one can deny that," I said.

"Do you really think anyone would want to fuck an old body like this, especially with one boob gone now?"

"Some like it hot, some like it cold . . ."

"You don't say."

"Some like it in the pot nine days old!"

"You can't be serious!"

"Why not? Why the fuck not?"

"Really, you are going a bit overboard there," she said.

She worked steadily at the painting for awhile and then she said lets break for tea so we walked into the kitchen.

"We only have this one teabag of Mr. Earl Grey left," she said

"I love Earl Grey," I said.

"Are you sure you're not bored to death sitting here?"

"I happen to love boredom," I said.

"My, you are a patient one, aren't you? I think I'm getting your head now. I think I'm finally getting your head right."

"Do you like my head?"

"A marvelous female head."

"I'm fishing for compliments," I said.

Returning to our seats in the bedroom . . . "look a little that way please," she said.

I turned and stared this time at all the pine trees and the forest blowing out the window.

"Do you have many lovers? You're so beautiful, you should be having hundreds of lovers," she said.

"I can't even remember when I had one."

"My, you can't mean that, I've had hundreds of lovers.'

"Tell me about your life, forget this nonsense about lovers," I said.

"Well, my mother killed herself and I had to go live with my aunt and uncle, and that was the start of a whole wasted life."

"Did your mother really kill herself? Why did she do that?"

"Because she was a bitch, that's why."

"How dreadful" Why did she do it?"

"Well, first my sister died. She got rheumatic fever and in those days no one knew what to do with rheumatic fever."

She immediately brought out a picture of her mother, looking like Virginia Woolf, flanked on either side by two beautiful little girls with large deep eyes. "You are the blonde child over here, aren't you? I can see already that your sister looks sick."

"My mother killed herself after my sister died. Then my father was killed."

"What a violent family! What happened then?"

"And then I went to live with my aunt and uncle, and they thought you ought to eat your vegetables before your dessert and brush your hair and do your homework and show that you know how to do things well, and I was miserable. I went to CAL and joined a sorority because my aunt said you had better chances to marry into your social class, but we had no social class and of course I was very lonely in the sorority and had no friends there and I kept looking outside the sorority for my friends. I kept bringing weird people home for dinner until finally they asked me to leave, which was lucky for me, and then my aunt was dreadfully disappointed in me."

"And that's when you married your first husband?"

"Indeed! A jackass thing to do, but I was too young to know that then."

"I understand," I said.

"Do you really understand? Or are you just in the habit of saying you do, which is it, I have my suspicions, you know."

"I don't know, I said. And then what happened?"

"Nothing happened. They were all very nice, all the husbands I ever had were all very nice, they were all lovely men, but I was just this silly woman who kept marching away from all of them."

"Well, it couldn't be that simple. People don't just march away when things are wonderful."

"Are you sure?" she said.

"Well, things are never that wonderful anyway," I said.

"Would you like another break now?" she said.

"Really, no, I'm fine, I could sit for hours, it's this pointless quiet."

"We do have Mr. Earl Grey waiting for us there in the kitchen."

"All right," I said.

"Shall we have some more cheese as well? I think I know your head quite well now, but I'm having a little trouble with your nose."

"I hate my nose," I said.

"I wouldn't hate it if I were you, it's a very nice nose, and your eyes are quite green, aren't they? Mr. Earl Grey has really had it by now, there's nothing left inside him, is there, he's all used up now, isn't he?"

Before we could laugh about Mr. Earl Grey, we went back to our respective seats. This time, instead of staring out the window at the trees, I returned to the pool of light on the Indian bedspread.

"So what happened with husband number two?"

"Husband number two, Mr. Crouton. He was an artist, poor thing, and he had no interest in sex after the first few years or so, and I felt that I had to have someone touch me, I could not do anything without being touched, and I said, John, what *is* the matter with you? Do you think artists can do their art so exclusively without needing to be touched at all? Why, what a silly woman I was to ask! I just didn't realize there are two types of artists, those that need it and those that don't. And those that don't just want to be locked up with their art, and husband number two was just that kind. Oh, he was very hurt when I got lovers, but I was working to support the child, that angry, depressed, miserable boy who is now 24 years old that you just met a moment ago, and I certainly needed more than to be locked up with my art. Well, it was then that I met husband number three, Mr. Ralph Cacciatorre."

"O, tell me what he was like, please."

"Husband number three was a business man and it looked like I had finally found someone to take care of me. He was rich, oh, we were not filthy rich, but we had a house, a swimming pool, a barbecue pit in which we pitted with the neighbors, and I just nearly died of it, I had no time to myself at all! And Mr. Cacciatorre, husband number three, he didn't understand any of this at all. "O you artists," he would say, "O you artists with your artistic temperament." But husband number two didn't know that people felt anything, he didn't even know that other people existed, he wasn't sure! And husband number three, he was worse, he thought that all people wanted to do was make money and pit in their backyard.

"I need time to be alone. I need time to wonder and time to be miserable and time to paint," I said, and number three said, "O you artists with your artistic temperament."

"What happened then," I said.

"Well, then I moved away from husband number three. Everyone thought I was crazy because I had a nice kind man to support me and he liked sex with me, we had very sensible, swimmingly sensible sexual times at our swimming pool, and pitting the barbecue or barbecuing the pit in our backyard with intelligent neighbors and everything, all the trimmings, but I just walked away and came to Berkeley . . ."

"How long have you been in Berkeley?"

"Forever, you fool. I'm dying to get out of here, but I simply don't have a dime. I've been telling myself that I should rent this miserable house and go to Mexico, I will paint in Mexico I tell myself, but the truth is I don't really feel like painting, I don't feel like going to Mexico with a lot of easels and brushes and painting all day, this is the first piece of work I'm doing right now, your face, since the dreadful operation in which I lost one boob, and since Max's father died last month, that's husband number two, the ill-fated Mr. Crouton. Maybe I'll get some money from his estate, such as it is. I have to see about getting over to Social Security, but now with the busses on strike, and not having a car. Everyone is waiting for those busses to get back again, aren't we, aren't we all waiting for those awful busses? Yes, husband number two, Mr. Crouton, called me up before he died . . . you know I'm still married to you," he said, "I was always married to you."

"But John! I said, you know I married Mr. Cacciatorre after you, you know I had another husband."

"Shit on that," he said. "That was a fucking illegal Mexican. divorce!"

"So husband number two and I were married at the time of his death, according to Social Security, and I may get something there. There's that to do, and then there's this awful house. First of all, it's splitting down the middle, it has to be jacked up every five years."

"So do I," I said.

"And that costs a couple of thousand dollars, and I'm sick of it, I have to meet some men, you know, but who would want me with this one boob gone now."

"No one, of course," I said.

"Oh you, you and Dr. Bingo. He is the most witty man, the surgeon, you know, he came to see me after the operation and he kissed me on the forehead and we talked as he changed the bandages those times I went to see him in his office. "How will anyone want me?" I said, and he laughed and laughed. "Don't be silly, you silly woman you, you just throw a scarf over the scars or something!"

"Don't you be silly, you silly Dr. Bingo, you! Anyone will want to see what's going on under the scarf, isn't that the truth?"

"And that kind, kind man keeps insisting that I wear a scarf over it."

"Well?"

"But, my dear, she said. If the scarf is beautiful, someone will want to touch it, someone will want to move it around to see how it is draped, to feel it, to see what it is covering, you can't go to bed with a scarf on."

"Scarves are an absolute must for going to bed with, haven't you heard?"

"Oh you, you and Dr. Bingo, she said. He *is* a witty man, I was lucky to get him. The first surgeon I went to see when I first heard this awful news that I would have to have my breast chopped off, I started sobbing in his office, I was feeling absolutely ghastly, I had just heard that Mr. Crouton, husband number two, had died, my child's father, and he had sent me all his junk, all his paintings and poetry and all his old PG&E bills, well, there I was being told that my breast had to come off and naturally I started sobbing in the doctor's office, and he said, "My, my, you really are getting hysterical, aren't you?" And I said, wait a minute, please! I don't want the likes of you cutting me up, he was shocked when I walked out of there, he thought I was just so goddamn down I had to take his superior doctor crap, isn't that the truth? I may be stupid, but I had the sense to know he was a disgusting man and I told him so."

"Aren't you the disgusting man!" I said, "I believe I'll go somewhere else thank you to have my tit removed." And that's how I found Dr. Bingo, I was one lucky person to find such a gentle, witty, sexy man. 'But how will I do it?'" I said to him. "Silly!" he said.

"I tell you my dear, all you need is a little drape"

"Really! You know it can't work that way, you know I'll have to tell the person ahead of time, I'm not in the habit of getting into bed with people and having them go all green with surprise on me. I don't think I'll be able to carry that one off, I may have already had the last fuck of my life."

"I believe I've had the last fuck of mine," I said.

"But this old flesh," she said. "Of course, if there's any communion, no one cares much, do they?"

"I fucked an old man once. It wasn't so bad, Fritz Perls, the father of Gestalt Therapy, when he was 76."

"You didn't!"

"Absolutely! And I was one of thousands, that old fart, he had a way with women. It wasn't so bad. His prick was out of order, but he had hands, he had a tongue, as a matter of fact, he had a very nice trick with his tongue."

"Now did he really? The dear man," she said.

"Yes, I believe he did."

"You know, your head is really looking quite a likeness now, I was always able to create a likeness and I have enjoyed spending this time."

"It has been very restful for me too," I said. "I have stared at that one pool of sunlight on your bedspread for hours now."

"But wasn't the old hanging flesh distressing?" she said.

"No, I wondered why afterwards, but it just wasn't, does that sound silly? I don't know, it was rather nice actually, remember, sex is first and foremost on the kinky side, don't forget that one."

"Really, you are too encouraging," she said. "You do want the best of things, don't you?"

"Something like that," I said.

In the meantime, the artist lady's son, Max, came down into the room where we were sitting. Max was the beautiful type, vicious and beautiful.

"May I have some money mother?"

"Where are you going?" said the mother.

"I'm going to Sixth Street," said the boy.

"Now what delightful thing is there on Sixth Street?"

"I need some money, mother," he said.

"Well, look in my purse and take what you want," she said.

The boy left, looking very pissed off.

"He's getting better. He used to hear voices, but now the voices are going away."

"Terrific!"

"I think he's sleeping with a boy, but that's his problem. I can't save him from himself, this boy, I do wish he'd leave me in peace, this motherhood thing is highly overrated, don't you think? It's actually a sort of little wasteland. After all this trouble, at this advanced and humiliated age, I still must find some way to support myself, M.A. in Painting, Master of Fine Arts, but what can I do with that? I tried running a workshop last year, I met Mimi Rabbit at her workshop, and she gave me all her materials, she'd had it as an Art Therapist, she was going to go get a Stockbroker's License instead. Then a kind man over at the Theological Union gave me five people who came to my class, I only had five, and four paying ones at that, hardly enough to make it worthwhile after you buy the paints and everything. I had them all make clay sculptures of their pain and the one who we picked was the shaman, and he drummed and drummed. The five people stepped on their pain and squashed it to pieces, things like that, oh dear, the afternoon is dying, the light's gone bad, will you come another time?"

"That's a possibility," I said.

"But is it a genuine possibility? You are a dear one, aren't you? You do want the best of things, don't you? I feel so old right now, you won't hate me for that too, will you? Tell me the truth, do you really believe that draping the scarf is a genuine possibility?"

* * *

lies

The man looked at his battery-operated watch and lit a Marlboro.

I love naked men smoking Marlboros, she made a mental note.

"I'm toxed, he said, I need a glass of carrot juice," walking toward the juicer.

The room semi-dark in one corner, the other, lit by high speed photographer's lamp, his balls silhouetted in the shadows. He made a joke about his watch "I can't move without my fascist wristwatch," he laughed. And then he said . . .

"What's the matter?"

"Nothing," she said, watching him move around his bestrewn apartment. "But aren't you getting a little too thin now?" she asked, observing his legs with a mild horror. He was now in his underwear, not the boxer shorts they sometimes wear, the other kind, jockey shorts that once were white, now a sickly yellow and ugly, hardly what the media showed a lover wearing.

"What is it with you, really, are you practicing middle-aged anorexia, or what?"

"You're just not used to people who know how to eat, he said. In the country of the blind, the one-eyed man is el sicko"

"One-eyed?"

"Yea!"

"Well, still and all, you should watch it, your thighs look like they're wasting away. I know men aren't supposed to have fat thighs, but yours . . . "

"What's eating you, something's eating you," he said.

"I'm worried about my daughter. (there's that) Also. I haven't had a good shit lately. My systems are all shut down, nothing's moving . . . And I think I'm getting fired from my job. Imagine, a Ph.D. in Art History, and I have a part-time job, with Foodstamps as a backup. My supervisor wrote me a bad evaluation, said I was a goof-ball."

"You're *sanpaku*," he said, "totally toxed. Anybody who knows anything just has to take one look at your face. It's those cappuccinos, and those restaurants. You pay a high price for being in the swim, or did you think you were getting a free ride?"

"Free ride? Where did I hear that before?"

He stood there with his yellowed jockey shorts, his very skinny thighs, feeding monstrously huge carrots into the juicer. It was making horrible noises, throbbing and shaking on the counter. He turned it off.

"It's overheating," he said.

"Why does my daughter have to dance so compulsively," she said, "does she really have such horrible feelings about herself? She called me up before, when you were in the bathroom. 'I had another wasted day Mom.' This in a tiny little baby voice. Fifteen years old, and afraid of time, 'I went to my ballet class today and then me and two friends, we went to have a mineral water in this greasy cafe, and another day was ended.'"

"The days always end, darling," I told her. "And you know what she said to me? 'You're too shleppy,' she said, 'you're a shleppy mother, you have no goals, so time means nothing to you, you don't mourn the passing of time because you've given up, there's nothing you want to do, but I'm different Mom, I don't ever wanna be like you, you'll never do anything with your life now, you're finished.' And she's only fifteen, how will she sound at forty?"

"Something else is eating you," said the man. "What is it?"

"Isn't that enough for you?" she said. "I'm divorced,

poor, middle-aged. Losing my job. Worried about my daughter. Under-employed. I can't have a decent relationship with anybody and I can't shit besides. I'm scared shitless, now I finally know what that expression means, when you're shitless, you're in trouble."

"I'll brew up a tea for you, and then you'll be able to shit," he said. "Senna. Lobelia. Cascara sagrada. Colon cleansers."

"I'll have to go home to shit, I can't shit here . . ."

"Are you afraid I'll hear you? Don't worry, I have a fan in the bathroom, it makes a lot of noise, you'll shut the door, and I won't be able to hear a thing you're doing in there."

"It's this day that's wrong," she said. "The walk we took in the park. And then the sex. X activity taking up X amount of time. I can't stand it. Linear time. Everything in its place, each in its own little moment. I need oceans. Oceans of time. Boundlessness. No beginnings. No ends. Everything a middle . . . like Chekhov says. A fuck that happens in spite of itself, the more insignificant the better. Sneaking up on you, sneaking away, without being noticed, like an unpopular person at a party. The sex was too deliberate."

"Is this another one of your feminist crap speeches?"

"Maybe," and she was still.

"You want my juices, don't you? You can't get by without the female juice."

"What the fuck is bugging you?" he said.

"You take my juices in your mouth, and when you're done, you spit them out in a glass. The glass stands next to your shortwave radio, which stands next to the bottle of rubbing alcohol, which stands next to your empty Vitamin C bottles. You save all your empty Vitamin C bottles, don't you? What's that all about, hey? I can't tell you how I feel when you spit my juices out into that glass."

"Thanks," he said, "mucho thanks."

"And besame mucho to you," she said. "It's true, isn't it? You want the juices, but you're too afraid of getting poisoned by them. You're afraid of Woman."

"Of all the shit, of all the goddamned rotten shit," he said.

"You want the juices of my heart, don't you? You only pretend to want my pussy-juice, but you really want the juices of my heart."

"How about both? Maybe I want both," he said. "But right now, I'll settle for a glass of carrot juice. Now, carrot juice, later for female nectar, I'm totally toxed."

He turned the machine on again, and started feeding

it the same monstrously large carrots as before. "I bought a 25 lb. bag of these in Priceless Foods last week, but I didn't realize they were too wide to fit into the juicer," he said. The machine started up again, making the same noise again, and overheating again, so he shut it off again. He came over to the single cot, his bed, where she was lying, covered by a hairy old Army blanket, and he put his hands through her hair and over the contours of her face. "Cheekbones," he said.

"I care for you a lot, but you lack true grit, you know? That's why you haven't worked. You told me it's been how long since you finished writing that book, your one book, *Underlying Idealism in German Expressionist Painting?*"

"Yes," she said, crying.

They were in a restaurant now, "hey, johnny one note, that's me," she said. She ordered a decaf cappuccino and a spinach salad, and he had grilled red snapper and a walnut and rhubarb torte.

"Look, I was reading something interesting," he said. "It was about this 75 year old violinist, playing for over 70 years. He's just formed a trio, the other two players are under 30. The interviewer asked, 'do you still practice?' The musician laughed. Of course, I practice, it is my way of getting air, the only violinist in the history of violin playing who didn't practice, who didn't have to practice, was Fritz Chrysler. He just tuned his violin strings, and just in that 50 seconds of tuning, he was already so attuned, that that was his practice. But he was a special kind of genius, not just a genius, mind you, but a special kind."

He was instructing her again, always the instructor.

"I love you," she said, very bored. "I love your words."

"Is that all?"

"That's enough," she said. "Words, the ultimate aphrodisiac."

"What about my bod? You've got the mind-body split," he said.

"Oh, you and your splits," she said.

"But our love, it must be situational. We can't love like 20 year olds. We're 48 and 50 respectively, we get constipated, have gum operations, worry about death. The doors are closing," he said.

"All right, so we'll love like old people. With sadness and memories, with appreciating of small things, nicely edged with doom."

He earned his living as a clerk in a spiritual bookstore. A middle-aged stockboy, his bitter joke. It had once been an intellectual street, street o' dreams, but now it was a crazy house, *la calle de los locos*. Schizoid types, gargoyles in rags parading around, wearing their red swollen feet as shoes . . . picking away in garbage cans, with total concentration! Their matted hair, stunningly offset by the highly visible presence of the good-hair babies, punky students and coeds all "into hair." Anti-static formulas, linoleic acid PH shampoos, style-setting gels, styling mousse, The Wet Look, dry, damaged hair the bugaboo. What was evil in the world? Damaged hair. If you counted both sides of the street, there were exactly seven hair places in two blocks.

The stories he had told her of taking on psychopathic street people when they tried to run their crazy numbers on him in the store, outrageous! The last story was about a six foot six black crazy who started up with a young Chinese girl with hair down to her ass who was in the store staring at Zen postcards.

The guy started whispering in her ear . . . "I wanna fuck you baby, I wanna eat your pussy out." The girl stood there traumatized, she just kept staring at the Zen postcards, using all her Chinese cool to not react to him.

Then the man took her beautiful hair in his hand, and with the other hand, started stroking it, all the time saying nothing.

"Not here you don't," I said.

When he told her that story, she loved him. She loved him for all his stories. He had the Jewish gift of storytelling, the gift for recognizing situations.

Oh, my darling, she said. I love you. You see things, I love you for the way you see, you sift, you sort, you taste. I, who am supposed to be a writer, I see nothing. I am brittle. I can only report. I can only stay close to the facts.

"Facts. Forget facts!!!!! Facts can be used in the service of nihilism. In contemporary capitalism, facts are merely nihilistic data. They don't tell you that in school, do they? We must depart from facts, like the plague."

Help me, help me to write again. Help me to depart, she said, from facts. Help me with my plague.

You mean help you with your nihilism! he said.

She cried and cried. He took out a handkerchief and wiped her nose. By that time, the waitress asked if they wanted refills.

When I first met you, I knew you were different. Especially when you squeezed that lemon for me right after my gum operation.

She was middle-aged. She had had the gum operation. She had stayed in the dentist's chair from 8 to 11:30 one morning. But he came to her when she called him. And he brewed her a strong blood-purifying tea. And she had only just met him, a short time before.

Really, he stayed barricaded in his apartment, "the bunker'" as he called it. "I'm king here," he said, "I don't need money. I don't need the dreck of this world."

"But then, how can you marry anybody," she said. "How can you take them out to dinner and a movie? What good is a boyfriend like you? Think of it, think of it from the woman's point of view."

"The women I want don't need dinners or movies. The women I want have to have experienced a personal holocaust," he said.

"You can't be serious!"

"Yes, a personal holocaust, to get along with me."

He just stayed in his apartment, with his short wave radio and his books, *Ancient Greek Verbs, Theories of Prime Numbers, Montaigne's Essays,* only the classical stuff, no dreck.

But he had come to her when she called. Infected gums, pain from the operation. Swollen glands, a bad headache. He had come to her apartment with a lemon and some golden seal.

"Flush the kidneys," he said. "When you don't know what else to do, flush the kidneys."

"What's that?" she said.

"You drink four hot cups of distilled water with a lot of lemon juice squeezed in them. That's for starters."

She asked for the check.

"Remember, always flush," he said. "This restaurant is shit. Bad food combinations. Phony crap. Nihilistic diversions."

"But don't we all need some diversion?" she said.

"It's all *dreck,*" he said. "All these so-called pleasures are to keep the nihilistic game going. You've got to give up the game and clean yourself out. Clean out the shit, he said. In your head and in your asshole."

Meanwhile, at the next table, there was a conversation, something like this. "You gotta get outa here, there's nothing for you in this city. This city is full of sad middle aged women, you're just getting a distorted view of your possibilities from this city, middle aged women, dazed as if poisoned, walking the streets. Portland, that's the place, the city voted the best city to live in. I'll get myself a condominium there, all in glass, on the 13th floor. Men came onto me there, I met a lot of men."

"Flush the Kidneys," he said. "Time is crushing me also. You're not the only one. It became time for you to stop writing, and now, it's my time to write. Don't be jealous of me."

"Let's go home and make love," she said.

"That is the most nihilistic remark I ever heard," he said. "You're jealous because I'm glowing and you're not. I know what to do with myself and you don't! You have to respect my writing. Sometimes you'll call me and I'll be unavailable to you. You must respect that, that's what I mean by situational. We're not kids anymore, we have to use our time. You must restrain yourself. There's other things for you to do besides your Jezebel act. Just because you can't write anymore! Your sexy act is just a cover for your desperation. You get turned on by my thin and gaunt Jewish essence. MY essence is showing, bones in the desert bleached white, Integrity, you see integrity and you want to fuck it, but it won't work. You have to find something to do, but you're too nihilistic. Your sex is nihilism in disguise, whatta disguise, it's the shit disguise of this entire crap culture we live in. Sex! As if anyone understands what it means!"

She was crying in her refill.

"I was very productive today," he said. "I started my book of aphorisms. I worked for four hours today, sitting in the window of Burgerland. Let's get outa here. I have to go home and take some very strong detox measures after this shit lunch."

She paid the bill, he never had money. Money wasn't his currency.

"Oh, there's someone I know. They're coming over to us to say hello," she said.

"I'm leaving. I don't have time for your nihilistic friends."

"You're being very crazy. Crude and patriarchal. You're not respecting me," she said.

He ran out of the restaurant, and she ran after him.

"You're not respecting me. You're too crazy," she cried into the street.

"What can you know about respect," he shouted, "a goddamned nihilist."

Everyone turned around and looked, two saggy middle persons with unfashionable clothes.

"A nihilistic person talking of respect! A contradiction, my dear. You have to douse yourself with poison to drown out your self-loathing, your self-loathing is asphyxiating even you! The media, in all its bestial nihilism . . ."

"Shut up," she was saying, "shut up. And yet I respect you, you stand for something. Ideals, like the German Expressionists. You're standing for something, though you are an asshole."

"Don't ever foist people on me again," he said.

"Who foisted? Someone just came over to our table."

"Don't call me, you hear? I'm doing some serious detoxing in the next two weeks. I'm staying home. Unplugging the phone. Don't bother me, you hear? Detox and write, you hear? No fucking, no relating, hear? I am writing, do you hear?"

"Yes," she said, "trying to catch up to him. Every morning you go and sit in Burgerland with your fountain pen."

"I'm writing," he said, "do you hear?"

"But why are you the only one still using a fountain pen?" she said. "How come you haven't heard about the ball point revolution? How come you can have such contempt for progress?"

". . . *Khub iss bakokt. khub iss in drerd,*" he said, running, crossing streets unsafely.

By now, traffic had stopped. He turned around, with his arm high in the air like Simon Bolivar on his horse.

"You! You do nothing. You are fundamentally unserious. A nihilist, you hear? The desire for movies and restaurants has destroyed your talent. Each day I sit in the window of Burgerland and write social commentary, you hear?"

"I thought it was aphorisms," she said.

By then, she caught up with him.

"They're the same," he said. "But I don't know what to do with these pieces, yes, that's the question, what to do with them."

"Well, take them and mail them away somewhere."

"I would do that, except the only thing that happens to me is I look at them and they look like crap," said Mr. Detox.

"That's called . . . getting a skill," she said.

By then they were at his place. "Look, how would it be if I did this detox with you?" she said.

"I must have at least three gallons of poison in my small intestine," he said, "with all the cokes I drank in my lifetime. I must've had at least 10,000 cokes, my prostate must be shot to hell. At least do something useful when I'm not around, read Kafka or Shakespeare, do the Sonnets. Then we'll have something to talk about next time we see each other. Then, at least we'll have a basis."

"That really hurts my feelings," she said. "I thought we already had a basis."

"Well, something to give it that little extra bit of richness. I phoned this herb store in the city today. I had this awful scene there with two people who own it, a year ago, but the older woman, she forgot about it. I called them and asked if they had Dr. Christopher's formulas. 'All of them,' they said."

"I wanna go on this detox with you," she said.

"If you did, you'd be beautiful. Years would fall off your face. The spots would disappear, anyone can see that you're toxed."

"But aren't you afraid you'll lose me if I get too beautiful?"

"I'll take my chances. Do you know how to give yourself an enema?"

"I'm afraid of enemas. My mother once tried giving me one when I was little."

"Trust me. I could give you one to start off."

"I'm afraid I couldn't do that," she said.

"You're so fucking conventional," he said. "You'd rather walk around toxed, pretending you're sexy, when there's a foul stench inside you. Your colon is loaded with shit, but you'd rather go to some restaurant and put more shit in there, and then to a movie, to put some more shit in your head, as if you don't have enough in there already. It's grotesque, your nihilistic priorities."

"Well, you're one helluva difficult boyfriend to have," she said.

"You! You want the same damn rotten lies you had in your marriage, the same stinkin' rotten lies, only more, more of the same, don't you? because you think there's nothing else! 'Am I sexy? Did you like it?' A little jocko, a little *shtupo*, a little il perverso. And you're jealous of my writing because I want to make a break with everything. You're jealous because I want to get the shit out of my system. Yesterday I wrote some damned good social commentary. If you were serious, you'd be able to write too, but your head is so full of shit, you can't think."

"It's not that I can't think," she croaked inside her heart, "I can't feel, which is ten times worse."

"If you were writing, you'd be ruthless with your time!"

"Oh, please stop attacking me," the woman said.

"I haven't even started yet. Who else will tell you the truth? Your nihilist friends?"

"Okay, so I'd be ruthless."

"You bring nothing but the philistine into my life. Fuck me, fuck me, do you love me, do you want me? It's grotesque, a parody of intimacy."

After a certain amount of abuse, she took leave of him and went home. She was happy to be alone and gorged on food. Two weeks went by, and no call. Two weeks without a fuck.

Then the phone rang. It was a woman friend.

"I've been two weeks without a fuck," she said to her

friend.

"Well, at least you've got somebody to fuck you sometimes. I can hardly even have a conversation with a man let alone sex," the friend said. "I'm jealous."

"At first, he was just a talking friend. I couldn't wait for him to become my lover. Fuck me, fuck me, I cried, you're tantalizing me with your talk, your global mind."

"It's global foreplay!" said the friend.

"But he keeps lecturing me on nihilism."

"Oh, they do lecture, that's the male thing."

"It's very frustrating."

"It's for power, I suppose. They love coherence. It gives them the illusion of something. I couldn't be coherent if my life depended on it. I'm done with coherence, and trying to produce the illusion of coherence."

"Would you say you were incoherent?" said the woman.

"I meditate. All I do is meditate. I can't take anybody's lectures. I can't absorb anybody's verbal output."

"It is awful," said the woman.

"No, it's wonderful for some people. But for me, I just can't stand it anymore," said the friend.

"I said to him, how did you get to be so global?"

"I listen to my shortwave radio," he said. "The BBC, you get global that way. Try shortwave," he said.

"Darling, darling, I love your mind," I said.

"Not only are you not global, you're not even regional," he said to me.

"A typical male, typical," said the friend. "Keep it up, you've got a good thing going. Does he want to marry you? I bet he wants to marry you already."

"As a matter of fact, he talked about marrying, but it all turned out to be a four hour lecture on the bestial media. 'The media . . . in all its bestial nihilism . . .' it began."

"You, you are a natural wonder," said the friend. "To be able to listen to all that is no small thing. That takes stamina. Everyday, I get up and run to the Tibetan Temple on top of the hill, and I lie under the prayerwheel for hours, meditating. That way, I can escape people's verbal output. The wheel makes a lovely sound, I find it very soothing, I don't even know why. Then, in the evening, I go back again for evening meditation, from five to six. Silk flags are flying overhead, beautiful flowers and incense. There's some very good energy there. Yesterday, as I was lying down under the prayerwheel, a young woman came up to me. "Did anyone ever give you instruction in how to lie under this prayerwheel?" she said to me.

"Instruction? No. I do it because I like it, a very good

sound comes out of it, well it is a little like fucking, as a matter of fact, it's like having a lover with no verbal output."

The two women started to laugh, and one nearly peed her pants.

"As far as what they call global, what they call global now will pass away," the friend said. "In 100 years, all these global ideas will be replaced by other global ideas."

"How I love being here with you and talking like this," the woman said. "I love women for helping me find my bearings, I love my woman friends. The men, I only suffer them for a little physical warmth. I see them above me in the shadows, their testicles hanging down, their penis juggernauting towards me in the night, fuck me, fuck me, I cry, in my little nihilistic heart. Such a tight little pair of testicles, so dry and tight, wrapped as it were, in a bat-skin, a bat-skin I do not understand. No, I don't love his verbal output, I love his Champion juicer. Two weeks ago, he told me about sentences. He's taken up writing, and suddenly, he's lecturing me on semicolons and Henry James. The story must move forward by sentences, he said. The story must go on. Not by digressions, but by forward-thrusting sentences.

"How male."

"He buys nothing. He knows how to live without money. 'Detox and didactics, that's what it's all about', he says."

"Meanwhile, I am back in his apartment, and my 12 year old calls."

"Mom . . . !!!! What are you doing there? Are you fucking?"

"No, I'm just drinking carrot juice and listening to the radio."

"You're lying!" she says.

* * *

this picnic you're having

At the Live Oak Arts and Crafts Faire, everyone was sleeveless and bare, showing a gorgeous shoulder or two, except for her, she was in a mildewed winter coat.

"Why are you in a wintercoat?" I said. "It's a hot day at a spring crafts faire."

"You, you know nothing," she said.

Other people passed, a middle-aged woman, large and blonde with a new baby at age 47.

"Scooby, how are you?" I said.

She stared into the crowd with stale eyes, filmed over with milky stains.

"Scooby, Scooby, I heard you were sick, what's wrong with you? Answer me, I'm your friend."

"Who told you I was sick?" she barked.

"Karen," I said. "I met her one day at the co-op. She was cashing a check to go see you in Napa."

"O," said Scooby. "What did she say about me?"

"Nothing, Scooby, nothing, she just said you were sick."

"You re lying She told you I was avoiding life and copping out in Napa, right?"

"Right. O, you're right, Scooby dear."

"Well, it's a goddamned lie, she's fucked up."

"But you're out now, none of that matters anymore, tell me how you are."

"Like shit," she said, "that's what. This country is shit. I can't live in this country. Come away with me to Hawaii, the people are beautiful. The people know how to live there."

"I can't Scooby. I have my lifetime here. I have my children to take care of."

"You're a shit too," she said. "You're a shit and you have to live in shit."

"Don't get mad at me, Scooby. I'm glad to see you."

"You're just like all the others," she said. "Come sit down, I'm getting dizzy standing, I get dizzy sometimes."

It was hard to find a place to sit down at that particular faire because all the spots on the grass had dog shit on them. But we found a place. There we were in the middle of the faire, sitting in grass, two middleaged hulks. Scooby put her head down between her knees.

"Scooby, are you all right, Scooby, are you there?"

She sat up and stared through me. Lukewarm sour

milk film glazed and dazed her eyes. Then, without a word, she lay down again in the corpse asana, her head in the grass, her eyes neutral as the sky, open to everything and nothing. And so time passed us by. Young people passed us by as well, in two's and threes, upright, walking, wearing their ethnic clothes. In the distance, a beat up VW bus with a large intelligent dog in the driver's seat, staring out the window, a young couple sucking in some Acapulco Gold behind a bush.

"We are now depressed and middle-aged," she said.

We sat there, Scooby and me, she in the corpse asana in the grass, and me thirty pounds too heavy. Youths trampled over us, all skinny and gorgeous. How come they never get fat, I wondered. You never see a fat one. I had just devoured three carob brownies and some passion nectar in a styrofoam cup, and I was still starving.

"Are you alone today?" said Scooby.

"I'm here with my youngest child, the afterthought," I said. "Her name is Lingo, I call her that because she talks so much, it's such good talk too."

Just then the child ran across the lawn to me.

"I'm very sick," said Scooby.

"I know, what happened to you?"

"The bottom just dropped out of everything."

"I know."

"You don't know. You think you know."

"I'm depressed too, Scooby. Maybe I do know."

"Yours isn't like mine . . . I'm all alone. I'm completely alone now," she said.

"I know."

"You don't know, you only think you know. What about you? What do you do everyday?"

"I take care of the children, they're still young."

"That's right, I forgot you have children. That won't last forever."

"That's why we have children," I said. "Look at that woman over there, the blonde one. She's 47, her sixth child."

"Children," said Scooby.

"Don't you have a son?"

"I'm all alone, I'm completely alone now," she said.

"Yes," I said.

"I'm all alone now, there's no one there."

"I know," I said.

"You don't know. Stop saying you know. You don't know. Wait till it happens to you, then you'll know. Shut up till it happens. I know many people," she said. "But they're not there."

"Yes," I said.

"I see you," she said.

"No kidding."

"You're identifying with my depression. Some people run away from it and some people identify with it. They use me to get into their own depression. I should charge money. I should send you a bill. Can I bill you?"

"Sure, bill me."

She gave my hand a squeeze, and I squeezed back, and then I pulled away.

"Where is your grown-up son now," I asked.

"He lives in Berkeley."

Just then Lingo said, "Mommy, come here, I want to show you something."

"Hi Lingo," I said. "I'm here talking to my friend."

"I didn't know you had a friend," she said. (O, these precocious children of Berkeley!)

"Sometimes, I see him," said Scooby.

"But do you ever diaper him, or anything?"

"He's grown up. He's a car salesman."

"Who are you?" said the child to Scooby, accusing.

"I'm Scooby, who are you?"

"Mommy, come here, I wanna tell you something. I'm changing my name to Veronica," she whispered.

"I'm Veronica," she said. "But I'm really Little Red Riding Hood, before she sees the wolf," said Lingo.

"He's been on his own for years now, he's 22, you know, he became a car salesman."

"Mommy, can we go now? I've been waiting for you and waiting for you and now I'm really getting tired, and soon I'll really be getting mad."

"What is it you want, Lingo?"

"I want you to come over somewhere with me. I wanna show you something," said the child.

"This is a very sick country," said Scooby, "a very lonely, sick country. You see all these people walking around? They look like they know what's happening, don't they? Flashing themselves, look at them, they're dying of loneliness like you and me. That's what drove me out of my house today, I told myself I had to see all the lonely people."

A stale-smelling sweat glistened on her gray face, gray as Einstein's brain.

"How come you know everything?" said Lingo to the gray-faced Scooby. "How come you know everybody's lonely? She's the smartest lady at the whole fair," said the child to me. "Look, I want you to come over there right now, "said Lingo-Veronica. "I'm tired of standing around listening to you two. I want you to come over there with me and see the puppets, right now."

"I can't go right now, I'm talking to my friend."

"She's not your friend, and she's not gonna do anything for you but give you a boring life. You're both just gonna give each other a boring life, when I have something nice and new to show you, like the puppets and you won't come."

"All right Lingo, all right."

"I told you my name's not Lingo, my name is Veronica."

"What made you change your name from Lingo to Veronica," said Scooby. "I would like to change who I am too."

"I just got tired of being Lingo, that's all."

"I'm tired of Scooby."

"Then change it to something else," she said.

"Maybe she's right," said Scooby.

"Do you ever see your ex-husband," I said.

"He's married, his wife just had a baby."

"A younger woman?"

"What else?"

"Of course, I said. What about your son?"

"He's a car salesman."

"Life is strange," I said.

"Imagine, a car salesman," she said. "I've been dancing for over thirty years, me, an anarchist my whole life, and he's a car salesman. But he's acting on the side, he'll come out of it, the acting will get him out."

Just then I noticed that my pants were soaked with blood.

Oh, my God, my pants are soaked through with blood, I whispered to the Live Oak Park Arts and Crafts Faire.

I wanted to get rid of Scooby and the child. I was wiped out, as usual. My periods had started taking a terrible toll on me, it was more like getting pneumonia, not a period, but I was afraid of getting rid of Scooby after coming on so interested in her, and I couldn't get rid of Lingo because she was my mother, I mean, I was her mother.

"Would you like to come with us?" I said to Scooby.

"Yes," she said, as if it mattered where she went, she could carry her blight with her anywhere.

So we walked along. The child brought us to a dark-haired young woman sitting at a wagon full of puppets, leather pouches and woven pillows. Lingo tried on the toucan on her right hand.

"And that one's a monkey from outer space," said the vendor girl, "see those things he wears on his head?"

Lingo put the monkey on the other hand.

"Groovy, you got to groove now," said the toucan to

the monkey.

"I'm turning black," said the toucan, "me and my whole family, we're turning black next week, we're all gonna be black and groove like the black people."

"People are too alone in this country, no one's there," said Scooby.

"Yes, yes," I said.

"Could you buy me a puppet?" said the child.

"How much are your puppets?" I asked the vendor.

"Two dollars apiece. I see these in the stores for $3.50, so you're getting a good price."

The child was on her fourth drama cycle.

"Could I have two?" she said.

"I don't have money," I said. "I just have money for one."

Lingo-Veronica tried on the bear and the dragon, the elephant and the gopher, and then the cookie monster.

"I want all these puppets," said Lingo-Veronica.

"She's very imaginative," said the puppet-lady.

"Yes, but my God, must you have all eight?" said I to the child.

"I can't make my show without all of them, there has to be a lot of different people dancing in my show."

What a pesty kid, I thought, but I had encouraged her

to fight for what she wanted, especially because she was a girl.

"Scooby, you were doing fine last time I saw you. You were dancing. You were giving all your dance lessons to all the children of Berkeley. No patterning to the children's movements, you said. Free movement. You were the freest of them all."

"The bottom just dropped out," said Scooby.

"Yes, and your boy became a car salesman."

"Yea, he became a regular car."

"Can I have all these eight puppets?" said the child.

"My God, Lingo, I don't have money."

"Let me see, let me look in your purse," and she grabbed my purse away from me.

God, this child was crazy. How did I ever get such a crazy child?

The young vendor gave me all eight puppets for $12. A regular bargain.

I asked Scooby if she wanted to come home with me. I was tired and had to meet my other kids. We all piled into her truck, alongside her genius-guru dog, Shlep, dog of wisdom and tears, and a small bag of fruit next to the stick shift in a bag.

"Come home with me," I said to Scooby.

She was eating a small wormy apple with a ferocious hunger.

"I'm depressed too, maybe we can help each other. I'm alone also. I have a weird scene with my husband. I have a husband, but I'm alone anyway. He's going out tonight. I could use some company."

Scooby stared out of the truck window, her yellow sleep-in truck, eating her wormy apple . . . an organic apple, I could tell.

"God Scooby, I don't think you're sick."

"I never said I was. Just depressed."

She drove the truck home to my house and there we were. Lingo played with Shlep, and then the other children came home, and they played with Shlep too. Then we cooked dinner and served it up in the livingroom. Scooby dished it out to the happy children. We let the TV stay on, and didn't worry if food dropped on the livingroom rug, at long last the livingroom had been liberated.

"I like it here with you," she said.

"Me too," I said. "You're helping me. I need another woman here with me. I need someone to help me cook. You like the kids. Let's get married."

"The kids are gorgeous," she said. "I'm not so depressed when I'm with kids."

"The kids like the dog, it's nice."

"We have to learn to help each other," she said.

"I like standing here in the kitchen with you," I said.

"We have to learn how to be there for each other," she said.

"You mean it?"

"Of course, that's basic."

"Is it really as simple as that?"

"What else," she winked, chopping up salad.

Scooby washed the dishes. It was a pleasure to see them stacked differently than my usual way. A simple change in the way the dishes were drying in the dish drain was enough to excite me.

"Come live with me," I said.

"Are you serious?"

"Sure, why not? I could used some help around here. You're alone. You dig the kids."

"But the dog, you said your kid was allergic to the dog."

"She is, but we could figure something out."

"Well, what exactly is she allergic to?" asked Scooby.

"Feathers and fur. Conflicts and shit. Dust, mildew, mold."

"You mean she's allergic to the dog hair, what if she

doesn't touch it?"

"It still affects her. It goes into the air. I don't know how it works. It all goes into the air."

Scooby slept on the couch. She drifted off to sleep in the middle of our conversation when I went to the kitchen to look for food. Coming back to the livingroom, there she was, fast asleep on the couch, deep, deep in sleep, wearing that coat of hers. The article I had given her to read was lying on top of her, "The Aging Woman" in the collection, *Sisterhood is Powerful*.

In the morning, she brushed the children's hair, then they brushed hers. We decided to go back to the faire, but first, the oldest child wanted to go to the garage sale next door. It was a man I knew up the block who I had once had a bad exchange with. That man had a woman with him in the house, Drina.

"Oh Drina!" Scooby knew her and threw her arms around her. Scooby hadn't seen her in years. "Oh Drina, Drina!" Drina was wearing jeans and navy blue clogs. She had just married the man and they were moving to Vancouver.

"Why are you moving to Vancouver?" gasped Scooby.

"To live," said the girl. "I met him, and he was pretty straight, and we got married. He's a good man. There are

THINGS, but we'll work them out."

The man was divorced with a girl child of 8 or 9 in a little house with one stained glass window. He was selling his enlarger, some straight 3-button suit jackets, and a bunch of yesterdays' paperbacks, stacked in Old Crow Whiskey cartons.

Drina introduced Scooby to the man.

"We're getting rid of all our shit," he said.

Scooby kissed Drina goodbye, and we left for the faire again, and I got sick again, it's those damned faires where everybody is having such a good time. I lay down in the shitty dog-shit grass; this time, it was a terrible migraine, and more period blood. More naked hippies trampled me. I just lay there bleeding, Scooby had many friends.

She kept running into teenage girls that had once danced with her when they were four. They all remembered her. She would kiss them and say, "are you still dancing?" and they all said "no" rather sadly, and . . . moved on in the slow, aimless procession; bearded men in shorts, walking alongside women, pushing them through the faire, stopped her, "Scooby," they cried, "How are you?"

"I'm okay," she said.

"Still dancing?"

"No, I'm not dancing anymore."

"What's the matter?" said one, staring into her eyes.

She stared right back with her sour-milk-film eyes.

"This is Helga," said the man, introducing the woman he was with, a woman over the hill in bright yellow pants.

"Scooby's been very active in the dance movement in this country," said the man, moving on.

"Scooby," I said, "you know many people, many people stop and talk to you, we cannot walk one minute without someone knowing you."

"Yes," she said, "they all know me, but they're not there."

"Who was that guy? The one with the beard and Helga with the yellow pants?"

"O him? He was a friend of my brother's. He's from New York, came out here, got involved in the Growth Movement, divorced his wife. Now all he does is march women through faires wearing yellow pants."

"O Scooby," I said.

"I went to bed with him a few times, but I couldn't stand him. He wasn't there. But he was hurt when I dropped him, so hurt."

The children had their faces painted and then we came home again and made supper all over again, Scooby liked dishing it out in the livingroom, we let the TV play. Right after supper, she drifted off to sleep on the couch again, in her coat. She looked like a frozen corpse buried in the snow in an old brown winter coat.

In the middle of the night, I went to get tea in the kitchen. There was Scooby, standing at the front door.

"Scooby," I said, "what are you doing?"

"I'm going home now," she said.

"But it's five in the morning!"

"Yes," she said.

"Are you all right??"

She held her head, and started sinking and swaying into the ground, just the way you'd expect a menopausal woman to sink and sway into the ground.

"Scooby, are you all right?"

"I think I'm fainting," she said.

I locked my knee between her legs to hold her up.

She farted.

Don't go home now. It's no time to go.

I led her back to the couch. I laid her down.

"I got this disease when I was in Mexico. Dysentery. It doesn't come back except when I'm emotionally disturbed."

"Can you see about it?"

"I started to take some tests at Kaiser, who do you see

there? Do you know anyone good?"

"I see Dr. Weinglass, I don't know if she's good."

"That's who I see, she seems to know what she's doing."

"Well, what did she say?"

"She said I have to take some tests, then I got sick."

She was shivering and sweating and fainting on the couch.

"How's your stomach?"

"It's rumbling," she said, looking straight ahead.

When I woke up in the morning, Scooby was gone.

* * *

"Scooby stayed with me this weekend," I said to Karen, "did she tell you? we had a good time together. Depressed people can help each other."

Karen was divorced with four kids. She had recently discovered abstract painting, she couldn't work at home though, her canvases were too big to fit through the door. She had taken breathing lessons to get calm, to learn how to breathe and to center herself, to find her true energy through breathing.. She had taken me home with her once before to show me her before and after paintings. Before, they were anxious, lots of blacks and reds, fierce angry strokes, anxiety paintings. But, after breathing, she had turned pastel and asymmetric, very Zen. "There's nothing wrong with Scooby," she said, "nothing except one thing."

"What's that?"

"She does not know how to be alone."

"Is that so??" I said.

"No, that is the truth. Scooby is strong. She is beautiful. She would be all these things if she could only not be so scared to be alone."

"Well, it is scary . . . And she is alone. She has no husband, she has no child."

"Haha," laughed Karen. "That aloneness I would love. I wish all my children would go away. I would paint all day."

"But maybe you have never been alone the way Scooby is. Maybe her aloneness is twice as strong as yours and mine put together."

"No, no, that is not the point. It is a cop out. You are copping out. Alone is alone, and that's all. What have you got in your shopping basket?" she said.

"Ginseng, for energy," I said. "Ten cents an envelope."

"Yes, yes, I want that," she said. "Someone told me about that. And halvah, chocolate-covered halvah. I want to take some of that home to the kids."

"God, you look so skinny," I said. "How do you stay so skinny?"

"This is skinny? This is disgusting fat," she said. "I was beautiful three weeks ago, you should have seen me then. Since then, I gained a whole lot of weight."

"I loved having Scooby at my house," I said. "The only thing that worries me is she's not well, she got dizzy, when she left, she nearly passed out against the wall. And she farted. She passed a vile fart while passing out, she said she picked up something in Mexico."

"Scooby's never even been to Mexico," said the abstract Karen.

A week or so later, I came home to find this note from Scooby in my kitchen:

Amanda,
Just stopped by to say hello. Have been down until yesterday, until I popped up. Am shaky, but on today. Sorry to miss you. Thought about you all week, but was too low to do anything about it. Am fine now, like a miracle. What a funny machine we people are. How are you? Do you

have my number? 865-2218. Love, Scooby. I was so incapacitated I couldn't pick up the phone.

> p.s. This picnic you're having looks good.

> p.p.s. Did you ever hear this poem, it's from Yeats:

>> The intellect of man is forced to choose
>> Perfection of the life or of the work
>> And if it choose the latter must refuse
>> That heavenly mansion
>> Raging in the dark.

I think you got some kind of heavenly mansion going on here.

* * *

In Berkeley's Green and Pleasant Land 270